# WARNING:

Don't open this story unless you're prepared to ugly cry, but also ready to witness a story of hope and new love, a love that was there all along, just waiting to turn from a whisper ... to a shout.

# Books by

# C.M. STUNICH

## Romance Novels

**A DUET**
*Paint Me Beautiful*
*Color Me Pretty*

**HARD ROCK ROOTS SERIES**
*Real Ugly*
*Get Bent*
*Tough Luck*
*Bad Day*
*Born Wrong*
*Hard Rock Roots Box Set (1-5)*
*Dead Serious*
*Doll Face*
*Heart Broke*
*Get Hitched*
*Screw Up*

**FIVE FORGOTTEN SOULS**
*Beautiful Survivors*
*Alluring Outcasts*

**MAFIA QUEEN**
*Lure*
*Lavish*
*Luxe*

**DEATH BY DAYBREAK MC**
*I Was Born Ruined*

**TASTING NEVER SERIES**
*Tasting Never*
*Finding Never*
*Keeping Never*
*Tasting, Finding, Keeping: The Story of Never Box Set (1-3)*
*Never Can Tell*
*Never Let Go*
*Never Did Say*
*Never Have I*

**STAND-ALONE NOVELS**
*Baby Girl*
*All for 1*
*Blizzards and Bastards (originally featured in the Snow and Seduction Anthology)*
*Fuck Valentine's Day (A Short Story)*
*Broken Pasts*
*Crushing Summer*
*Taboo Unchained*
*Taming Her Boss*
*Kicked*

**ROCK-HARD BEAUTIFUL**
*Groupie*
*Roadie*
*Moxie*

## Violet Blaze Novels

(MY PEN NAME)

**THE BAD NANNY TRILOGY**
*Bad Nanny*
*Good Boyfriend*
*Great Husband*

**BAD BOYS MC TRILOGY**
*Raw and Dirty*
*Risky and Wild*
*Savage and Racy*

**TRIPLE M SERIES**
*Losing Me, Finding You*
*Loving Me, Trusting You*
*Needing Me, Wanting You*
*Craving Me, Desiring You*

**HERS TO KEEP TRILOGY**
*Biker Rockstar Billionaire CEO Alpha*
*Biker Rockstar Billionaire CEO Dom*
*Biker Rockstar Billionaire CEO Boss*

# Books by
# C.M. STUNICH

**STAND-ALONE**
*Football Dick*
*Stepbrother Thief*
*Stepbrother Inked*
*Glacier*

## Fantasy Novels

**THE SEVEN MATES OF ZARA WOLF**
*Pack Ebon Red*
*Pack Violet Shadow*
*Pack Obsidian Gold*
*Pack Ivory Emerald*
*Pack Amber Ash*
*Pack Azure Frost*
*Pack Crimson Dusk*

**ACADEMY OF SPIRITS AND SHADOWS**
*Spirited*

**HAREM OF HEARTS**
*Allison's Adventures in Underland*
*Allison and the Torrid Tea Party*

**SIRENS OF A SINFUL SEA TRILOGY**
*Under the Wild Waves*

**THE SEVEN WICKED SERIES**
*Seven Wicked Creatures*
*Six Wicked Beasts*
*Five Wicked Monsters*
*Four Wicked Fiends*

**HOWLING HOLIDAYS SHORT STORIES**
*A Werewolf Christmas*
*A Werewolf New Year's*
*A Werewolf Valentine's*
*A Werewolf St. Patrick's Day*
*A Werewolf Spring Break*
*A Werewolf Mother's Day*

**OTHER FANTASY NOVELS**
*Stiltz*
*Gray and Graves*
*Indigo & Iris*
*She Lies Twisted*
*Hell Inc.*
*DeadBorn*
*Chryer's Crest*

## Co-Written
(With Tate James)

**HIJINKS HAREM**
*Elements of Mischief*
*Elements of Ruin*
*Elements of Desire*

**THE WILD HUNT MOTORCYCLE CLUB**
*Dark Glitter*
*Cruel Glamour*

**FOXFIRE BURNING**
*The Nine*
*Tail Game*

**OTHER**
*And Today I Die*

# Baby Girl

C.M. STUNICH

INTERNATIONAL BESTSELLING AUTHOR

*this one is dedicated to Dollie.*

*rock on, girl.*

# EMBRY

## PROLOGUE

Something is wrong.

I know it; I just can't put my finger on what or why. My best friend, Phoenix Benoit, glances my way with his brow raised, pale blonde hair catching the golden rays of the dying sun. We're standing in the front yard, off to the side of my parents' cars so my mom doesn't catch him smoking. She never says anything when she sees Phoenix with a smoke between his full lips, but that woman knows how to send out waves of disappointment without even opening her mouth.

"Codrick should be here already," I say as I cross my arms over the shimmery pink of my mermaid dress. "He's been waiting for this night like a kid at Christmas. He's more excited about prom than I am." Glancing over my shoulder, I check to see if my mother's peeking at us out the window. When I see that she's not, I turn back to Phoenix, pluck the cigarette from his fingertips and take a long drag.

*1*

He smirks at me, crossing his muscular arms over his chest. For an eighteen year old, he's seriously ripped, much bigger than my fiancé, Codrick Landry. Since Phoenix lives in the bayou with his dad, we always joke that there must be something in that swamp water that's bulking him up. He's like the friggin' Hulk.

"He'll be here, *mouche a mielle*," he grumbles, his voice thick and heavy, almost like a purr. And with that Cajun accent of his? No wonder the girls at school are all over him. They have been for years, since junior high really. It took me and Codrick ages to get him to actually go out with someone. Yet, despite our pushing, he still doesn't have a date to prom. Instead, we're going as a group of three.

Doesn't bother me. My sisters have been teasing me mercilessly about it, but Codrick is the love of my life and Phoenix is our best friend, has been since we were kids. Hell, I'd marry them both if I could.

My mouth twitches and I laugh at the same time I cough. I don't smoke much and holy crap, my lungs are burning.

"What you thinkin' about over there, you?" Phoenix asks, dressed in a sharp black suit. It sits nicely against his sun-kissed skin, an intriguing dichotomy of rough-and-tumble bad boy mixed with the clean professional lines of his clothing.

"Nothing," I say, passing back the smoke. My fingers tangle with Phoenix's, but I'm too distracted by the fact that Codrick isn't here to pay much attention to the strange sort of spark that happens between us when we touch. I've always felt that with Codrick, always. From moment one, I knew he was meant to be mine. And Phoenix … I love Phoenix like nobody else in my life except for Rick. The Three Musketeers, that's what we are. They're my family before family, really. I know sure as shit that I like these two men more than I like my own sisters.

To be fair, my sisters are bitchy as hell.

"He wouldn't miss this for the world, no," Phoenix whispers, his eyes focused on the empty field across the street from my parents' place. There used to be a trailer park there, but it burned down and nobody bothered to come back. My parents were smart—when firefighters were still damping out the flames, they put in an offer on this lot and got it for pennies on the dollar.

Now, there's a glorious empty field, the grasses bathed golden in the strange gray-orange light of the stormy afternoon sunshine. The edge of the property dips into marshy water that then morphs into an old cypress forest. It's one of the most beautiful things I've ever seen.

"Should I text him?" I ask, but I always try not to bother Codrick when he's driving. He has a tendency to check his messages and I don't want him to crash. I told him he's not allowed to die until we're old and gray; almost everyone thinks we're idiots for getting engaged in high school, and I want to prove them all wrong.

"He said he was stopping to get flowers," Phoenix says, pulling his phone from his pocket and flashing the screen in my direction. "I bet he stuck at the florist, that *couyon*. He lets everyone and their Maw-Maw talk his ear off."

"He's getting flowers?" I ask, feeling my cheeks flush. As soon as Phoenix sees the color pink up my cheeks, he grins, big white teeth in a handsome face.

"You can't be that surprised, bumblebee," he says, using the nickname *mouche a mielle* in English this time. "Dat boy would do anything for you." He rises to his feet, this gentle giant with huge biceps and a wide chest. You haven't really lived until you've gotten a hug from Phoenix Avit Benoit. "Let's go get his ass. If we pass him on the way there, he'll see us."

Phoenix gestures over at his bike with his chin, just as tiny droplets of rain begin to fall.

Damn it.

My hair is shellacked to high hell, scraped back and twisted in all these fancy curls. If my mom or my sisters

find out I've climbed on the back of some boy's bike in my prom dress, they'll freak.

Hmm.

But screw it.

This is *my* night, not theirs. I let them dress me up, but there's nothing in the world like feeling the wind on my face, my arms wrapped around my best friend's waist, my cheek pressed against his back …

"I'll drive careful, me," he says, passing over a helmet and a leather jacket.

And well, fuck it. My heart is racing, and that awful feeling sitting my stomach is making me sick. I just want to find Codrick and get to the dance so I can relax a little.

Phoenix helps me slip into the jacket and then plops the helmet on my head, tucking strands of dark hair inside it.

"Hold on tight, Embry," he tells me with a wink, and then I'm hopping on the back of a motorcycle, my pink dress whipping in the wind behind us as big fat drops begin to fall, spattering against the helmet and making me feel so … alive.

Too bad that feeling doesn't last.

—————

The drive into town isn't far, but it's already late, the velvety fingers of darkness tracing across the sky as the rain comes down and soaks me and Phoenix both. And *shit,* is it cold. But holy crap, Phoenix is warm.

I cling to him as we speed down the quiet country road. We don't pass any other vehicles; not a lot of people live out here and the ones that do are probably already home from work.

Ten minutes down the road, I see headlights, crooked headlights.

That awful feeling in my gut twists and writhes like a snake.

"Pull over!" I scream, but Phoenix is way ahead of me, moving his bike across the empty lane and over to the side of the road. I'm off and stumbling before he even shuts his motorcycle off, tripping on my dress as I make my way toward the car.

The headlights are so bright, they sting my eyes and make me squint, but even with the hot glare bathing me, I can see that this car ... it's upside down.

*It's not Codrick,* I tell myself as I get closer. *It's not because it can't be.*

It can't be.

I'll die.

I'll fucking die.

But as soon as I step out of the headlight beams, I see the cherry red paint of Codrick's Toyota Corolla and my heart explodes inside my chest, pieces splattering against my ribs as I tear off the helmet and toss it aside.

I drop to my knees in the gravel, not caring that bits and pieces dig into the thin, wet material of my dress and stab me. Falling forward, I lean my cheek against the ground to peer inside … and my entire world comes to a horrific end.

"Rick?" I choke out as Phoenix slides to the ground next to me, shouting something that I can't hear. The rain … disappears. The cold. The ticking, steaming sound of the engine. Emotion chokes up my throat just before a white-cold wave of shock sweeps over me. "Rick?"

Reaching out a trembling hand, I touch the bloody side of his cheek as Phoenix reaches in and tries to unhook him from his seat belt. He's upside down, Codrick is, just hanging there in limp silence. There are rose petals all over the car and as Phoenix gets him unhooked and drags him out, I see those glassy brown eyes looking into mine and I know that this is a moment I will never forget.

It's a defining tragedy.

A wound that will never heal.

It's a nightmare.

No, no, more than just a nightmare … because it's one I'll never wake up from.

Phoenix drags our best friend, my love, my fiancé, my soul mate, out of the car and lays him on his back, checking for a pulse with shaking fingers. As rain spatters us and I sit up, dressed in pink sequins with my hair plastered to the sides of my face, I see the roses clutched in Codrick's hand.

Red roses.

As red as his blood.

*No.*

No, this isn't how our love story ends.

It was just beginning.

This is our *beginning.*

Turning to the side, I throw up the bit of sweet tea I drank earlier. I was too excited, too nervous to eat anything today, so not much comes up, but my stomach tightens and squeezes, making me puke until it's bile and saliva that comes up.

*I love you, Baby Girl.*

That's the last text I got from Codrick. *Please don't let it be the last words we ever exchange. Please, please, please.*

Turning back to Phoenix, I see this look on his face, this broken, haunted sort of look that turns him into a stranger. I don't even recognize this man in front of me.

Who is he?! Who the fuck is this ghost of a human being?!

"I gotta grab my phone, Baby Girl," Phoenix chokes out, reaching out for my arm. I jerk away from him and look down at Codrick. He's bleeding and Phoenix isn't giving him CPR. Why isn't he giving him CPR?!

"Make him breathe!" I scream and Phoenix closes his eyes tight for a moment, shrouding the pain in his gray irises before he opens them back up and looks at me across the still, bloody form of Codrick's body. Droplets of rainwater are falling into his glassy eyes as they stare up at the sky.

*That must hurt,* I think as I reach out and pull them closed.

"Do the chest compressions," I tell Phoenix, leaning forward, but he reaches out with both hands and grabs my upper arms. His touch is firm but gentle at the same time. He shakes me a little and meets my eyes.

"He's dead, honey," he chokes out and I swear to God, I feel those words like a spear through the chest. "He already gone. I gotta get my phone; you come wit' me."

"He isn't dead!" I scream, tearing myself from Phoenix's grip and leaning down over Codrick, putting my ear to his chest the way I've done so many times before, listening to the gentle soothing beat of his heart, the comforting up and down of his breathing. "He isn't dead," I groan, repeating those words inside my head a hundred times over.

*He isn't dead; he isn't dead; he isn't dead.*

See, Codrick can't be dead because if he's dead then … I'll die, too. I'll die and Phoenix will die, and everything will fall apart.

"Oh God," Phoenix says as I hold Codrick's body close and listen to the horrible silence. Even through the pouring rain, I can tell he's not breathing. He's not breathing. He's not fucking breathing. "C'mere, Baby Girl," he whispers, reaching down for me.

Automatically, I slap his hand away and cuddle closer to my soul mate's body.

I stay there with my eyes closed, shielding him from the rain, praying that I'll wake up sometime soon, that I'll find myself under the covers with Rick behind me, his naked body pressing hot and hard against mine.

Because he's always hot, never cold. And right now, he feels cold. That's how I know this can't be real.

Phoenix stumbles back over and falls to his knees next to me. I glance up and realize that he has my cell instead of his own.

*Oh, isn't it lucky I got the waterproof phone?* I think absently, feeling like I'm swaying even though I'm staying still. *He must be using my phone instead of his*

*because of the rain. What a smart choice. That's a smart, smart choice.*

My best friend makes a call with shaking fingers, but I can't hear what he's saying. I can't hear anything but the beat of my own heart inside my head. Blood sloshes between my ears, making me deaf to the world. How funny this story will be when I'm sitting beside Codrick in his hospital bed, stroking my fingertips over the back of his hand. We'll laugh about how I couldn't hear anything at all, how Phoenix had to call an ambulance because I fell apart.

And oh, wow, how I always thought I'd prevail in the face of tragedy.

How silly, that I should fall apart.

Isn't that funny?

It's funny, right? So fucking funny.

I start laughing as I sit up and Phoenix freezes, staring at me with eyes so wide they look like Codrick's did before I closed them. I laugh and laugh and laugh, and then when Phoenix grabs me and holds me close, those laughs turn into sobs.

My fingers find Codrick's hand and close around his still, cold fingers, knocking the roses aside and scattering more petals.

Phoenix … is warm in all the places that Codrick is now cold.

A wail escapes my throat as I bury my head under Phoenix's chin and scream.

By the time the ambulance arrives ... my throat is shredded and raw.

And so is my heart.

■ ■ ■ ■ ■ ■ ■ ■ ■ ■ ■ ■ ■

My pillow is stained with tears and my eyes feel like sandpaper. For days—I'm not sure how many—I've laid here and cried. My parents have come and gone; my sisters stay away. Phoenix is an eternal presence, sometimes sitting in the chair in the corner, sometimes cuddling up against my back and making me feel for a moment like Codrick is right here with me.

There are these moments, few and far between, where I wake up and for an agonizingly short period of time, I forget that Codrick is dead. My jumbled mind tells me it's him in my bed, creating that indent behind me, one arm thrown over my body and holding me close. And oh, God, the sound of that heartbeat, that rhythmically perfect heartbeat. The sound of it touches me in deep places, making me smile before ... I start to cry again.

Because as soon as the bubble of sleep breaks and the reality sets in, it's like Codrick is dead all over again.

I'm wrapped in the hoodie Phoenix slipped over my head ... two days ago ... three? I can't remember. I don't know how long it's been since ... fuck. As soon as we got back to the house, I tore my wet and bloody dress off, balled in up and shoved it into the sink, dressed only in black lingerie and hyperventilating until I thought I might pass out.

And then there Phoenix was, giving me a hoodie that smells like him, and sweats that smell like him ... and yet all I want to do is lie here with one of Codrick's shirt pressed to my face.

"I want to die," I tell Phoenix. It takes him a moment to stir, early morning sunshine peeking in through the window. Now that I'm more alert, I've just remembered that the funeral is today.

The funeral.

Codrick's funeral.

Lifting my hand up, I examine the small diamond ring he gave me. It's an inexpensive cut, but I don't care. I've never cared about anything like that. The only thing I ever cared about was Codrick, and now he's gone.

I'll have to live a whole life without him. The only way I can even think to make that thought less painful is to make the life I live shorter.

"Don't talk like dat," Phoenix says, burying his face in my hair. I haven't seen him cry since he was ten years old, and yet ... over the last few days, I've had these horrific moments where I lie awake and listen to him weep softly from the chair. "You too good for this world." He reaches over and swipes some hair off my forehead.

"What's the point?" I whisper, my voice shaking as I slip the ring off my finger and set in on the windowsill. I can't wear it anymore; it feels like it's burning my skin, searing my flesh from my bones. The light catches on the tiny diamond and casts prisms over my face. "I just don't see the point without Codrick ..."

"I got you, *ma 'tit fille,*" he whispers, pressing a kiss to my cheek. I barely feel it. There's too much pain inside of me, too much hurt. It feels like nothing good, nothing positive, nothing pleasurable will ever touch my heart again. "I got you, and we'll get through this together. If you need to, you lean on me, you hear?"

Closing my eyes, I push up from the bed and feel my head spin. I've had barely any water, haven't touched any food for days. I don't care if I never eat again. I could starve to death and it wouldn't even hurt because I don't care. My life ... is nothing now.

Nothing.

Pushing off of the bed, I stumble and Phoenix is right there to catch me before I fall.

"You want me to run a shower for you, *cher*?" he asks, but I shake my head. I don't care if I smell, if I look like shit. None of that matters.

As I pass by my desk, I can see the acceptance letter for NYU where Codrick, Phoenix and I were planning to go after graduation. Codrick and I got in, but Phoenix didn't. We'd decided as a group that we'd all go together anyway. The thought of being split up ... hurt too much.

Now, fate has made that choice for us, torn my soul in half and left me a broken fragment of a human being.

"Da funeral's in about two hours," Phoenix says tiredly from behind me. Shoving his sweats down my hips, I sit on the toilet and pee. I don't care if he's looking. I don't care about anything anymore.

Gentleman that he is, he turns away and leans his back against the wall.

"Take me there," I say tiredly. "Take me now and we'll wait."

With my eyes staring blankly at the gray-blue wall in front of me, I try to decide if I really have the courage to kill myself. Because it's the most dichotomous truth in the whole world: taking one's life shows both extraordinary amounts of bravery and infinite levels of cowardice.

A sob bubbles out of my throat and I lean forward, putting my forehead on my naked knees. As good as that darkness would feel as it closed around me, I know in my heart that I can't leave my parents or my sisters … that … I won't leave Phoenix.

His soft sobs haunt my mind like specters, and I imagine that if I died today, the day of his best friend's funeral, that he might not make it either.

But … dead … and gone can be two different things.

That letter floats in the forefront of my mind. It's an escape. Escape. I can run from all of this.

Suddenly, my skin feels itchy and the urge to run hits like a tsunami.

After the funeral … I'm going to pack up my stuff and leave.

And I'm never—*never*—going to come back.

■ ■ ■ ■ ■ ■ ■ ■ ■ ■ ■ ■ ■

The cemetery is the worst place in the world.

I hate it.

"I don't want to go over there," I tell Phoenix, sitting on a bench two rows down from the Landry family tomb. All the crypts here are aboveground—they have to be because of the marshy land and the high water table —with big strips of grass between the graves.

The funeral is taking place now; I can hear the sermon from here. But I don't make any move to get up and

neither does Phoenix. What's the point? Codrick is dead, and he's never coming back. I just don't think I can stand to see his mother sobbing anymore, talking about how God must've needed another angel in heaven.

I don't believe any of that shit.

If God really does send teenage boys to their deaths on the side of the road, roses clutched in hand, rain falling from the sky in fat, cold drops … then really, he's just the second face of the devil.

"You don't gotta do anything you don't want," Phoenix says, sounding tired and worn-out. I've never seen him like this before, not even on days where his dad gets drunk and pushes him around. He looks like a shell. It's pretty on the outside but on the inside … there's nothing but a hollow core where something used to live.

Rocking forward, I choke back another sob. I'm not going to cry anymore. I'm not going to shed a single tear ever again. Because after this, there won't be a thing left that's worth crying over. I've decided that for the sake of the people in my life, I'm going to drop this shell in the ocean and let the waves carry it off. I won't crush it or destroy it; I'll just let it float away.

It's the best I can do.

And I assure myself that if I ever drift so far that they can't see me anymore … maybe I'll end it then.

"He loved your more than he loved himself, you know dat, you?" Phoenix asks softly, but I can't look at him. Instead, I stare blankly ahead, at a patch of brown grass amongst all the green. Dead and lifeless. Shriveled. Destroyed.

"I know," I whisper, but that thought doesn't bring me any comfort.

Codrick loved me more than the world, and I loved him right back.

That didn't stop him from dying.

That didn't stop him from bleeding to death on the side of the road. Or hell, maybe he died on impact? I don't know. I don't care to ask questions or find out. Because dead is dead.

It's the one irreversible truth in this world.

Before, it was my greatest fear, losing Codrick. And now, death is my greatest wish. It's the only thing bringing me comfort, knowing that someday *I* will die and be able to join him.

I've gone from upbeat to morbid in less than a week.

"I love you, too, you know?" Phoenix says, and I get the feeling he's reaching out to me, seeking something. He needs comfort, too, I know that, but I'm just not sure if I'm strong enough to give it to him. Turning on the bench, I stare at him, at the dark shadows under his eyes and the pain in his gray gaze. "I love you so much, Baby

Girl," he says … and … something inside of me snaps. Cracks right in half. Breaks.

My eyes widen and my heart starts to pound.

*I love you, Baby Girl.*

The last words Codrick ever said to me.

"Don't," I say, standing up and backing away. My voice is trembling so bad that it doesn't even sound like me anymore. It cracks and breaks, shatters like glass and tears me apart from the inside out. "Don't say that," I growl, tripping over the edge of a tombstone and falling hard on the raised cement grave.

Phoenix comes toward me to help, but I slap his hand away, my eyes so wet with tears that he's nothing but a blur in the sunshine.

"Don't say what?" Phoenix asks, dropping his hand and falling to his knees on the grass in front of me. I swipe away the tears I refuse to shed, channeling some of my pain into anger that Phoenix doesn't deserve.

"Baby Girl! Don't say those words *ever* again," I snarl out, scrambling to my feet, breathing so hard that everything around me flickers white, my vision shattering as I struggle against a sudden lightheadedness. "That's *his* name for me," I spit as rebel tears sting my eyes, desperate to get out. "You're trying to replace him! He can't be replaced! Stop trying!"

"I would never," Phoenix starts, but I'm turning and running away from him.

Running *from* him when I should be sprinting towards him. He's in pain, too; he's hurting, too.

I know that, but …

I find my mother and dig her keys from her purse, probably drawing the attention of everyone at the funeral, but there's not a single part of me that cares. Heading over to her car, I climb inside and see Phoenix watching me from the grassy knoll next to the gravel road. His gray eyes penetrate into the very deepest parts of my soul, but I'm too broken inside now. I hurt too much.

"I love you," I tell him and Codrick both, and then I start the car and head home, burn my prom dress, and take off for NYC.

I promise myself I'll never go back.

But not all promises can be kept.

And sometimes … it's for the better.

# EMBRY

## CHAPTER ONE

*A year and a half later ...*

I shouldn't have come back here.

That's my first thought when I park the car in the driveway and open the door. I don't even have to get out before I know I've made a mistake. Heart pounding, I put one foot on the gravel driveway, staring at the toe of my gray suede boot. A single raindrop falls, and then another, like tears from a weepy sky.

"Fuck," I curse, grabbing my duffel bag off the passenger seat and climbing out of the car. I slam the door behind me and take off running for the front steps, flying up them and into the—*relative*—safety of the porch. I say relative because there are holes everywhere, drip-drip-dripping into rusted metal coffee cans.

There's an awkward moment where I just stand there, staring at the wreath on the front door, its green tinsel arms threaded through with Christmas lights that don't work anymore. Do I knock? Do I go right in? I spent my whole life in this house. In fact, I've only spent four hundred and twelve days with a different address.

Nineteen years of life ... and only one of them away from this place and I don't know if I should go in or if I should knock or ...

The door swings inward before I get a chance to make that decision, my mother's gently lined face grinning out at me.

"Come on in, darlin'!" she says with far too much enthusiasm. Four hundred and twelve days with a different address and I haven't seen her in ... four hundred and twelve days. My mom pushes the screen door out toward me and I know I should smile back, but I haven't smiled in four hundred and sixteen days.

I'm not about to start now.

"Hey Mom," I say, slipping inside to the warm smell of freshly baked cornbread and collard greens with bacon, the murmur of boiling oil from the fryer and the distant mumble of the living room TV.

Stepping back into that house ... is like stepping into a time warp.

My throat gets tight and my vision goes hazy for a moment; the bag drops from my fingers as I struggle to control a wave of emotion.

"You okay, honey?" Mom asks, but ... I'm not okay.

Baby Girl

I haven't been okay for four hundred and sixteen days.

As I stand there, my vision swims and I rock back and forth on my feet for a moment.

"Yeah, I'm fine," I say, blinking away the pain and the memories. There's a giant lump still caught in my throat, and I'm finding it ridiculously hard to breathe, but ... I'll survive. I think. I mean, I've made it this long, why not just keep going? "When are we going to go see Dad?" I ask, because that's why I'm here, to visit my father in the hospital.

He had a minor heart attack ... and also, I have a paper due on grief so ... why not kill two birds with one stone? My psychiatrist thinks it's a brilliant idea. Standing here now, it feels like the worst idea I've ever had in my life.

"As soon as your sisters get here," Mom says, wiping her hands on her apron and watching me with a honey-brown gaze rife with sympathy. I hate that, that look that says there's a reason to feel sorry for me. All it does is remind me how things are supposed to be, how they should've turned out.

*"I married my high school sweetheart. Nobody believed in us, but your daddy and me ... Oh, honey, I know you and Codrick are gonna make it together.*

23

*You've got that special something that you just don't see every day. I can feel it."*

"Do I have time for a shower?" I ask, because I drove all the way down here, New York City to fucking Donaldsonville, Louisiana and I stink. I stopped one time—just once—and slept in a crappy motel, washed my hair, changed my clothes. But just once. If I made anymore stops than that, I would've turned around and gone right back.

I used to be a small-town girl—okay, a *sassy* small-town girl—but now … the anonymity of New York City suits me better. It's easier to push the feelings back there, let them be crushed under the buzzing weight of humanity. There are so many people loving and hating and hurting and crying that it makes my feelings seem less significant.

Seem.

They only seem that way. I know my feelings are big enough to encompass the whole world, drown it in my grief and carry everything else away.

I just don't let them.

"Sure thing! Fresh towels are in the hall closet like always! Oh, and we set up the den for you, darlin'. Just throw your things in there." She moves into the kitchen as I haul my bag's strap up to my shoulder and start down the narrow hallway in the back of the house.

While the outside looks pretty worse for wear—a sign of my father's struggling health—the inside is as homey and comfortable as it ever was. My mother is an incredible homemaker.

I move across the new wood floors in the hall—there used to be carpet—and find myself pausing next to a door I really don't want to pause at.

Before I can stop myself, my hand reaches out on impulse, feeling the familiar knob beneath my palm, the metal worn away from countless twists, countless moments frozen in time. I shove the door inward and … there's a room with freshly painted lavender walls, an elliptical machine, and a table pressed against the right wall with a sewing machine on top of it.

My bed is gone; my dresser is gone; all the things *he* gave me are gone.

"Mom," I ask, and my voice cracks slightly before I get it under control, turning back down the hallway and into the kitchen. She's standing over the stove with her back to me, dark brown hair gathered in a loose, messy bun.

They haven't gotten rid of the table. The *same* fucking table is here.

I stare at the yellow legs and try not to feel like I'm going to throw up.

"Mom, where are all my things?"

25

She pauses with a glass pan of cornbread in her mitt covered hand, glancing back at me with a stray tendril of hair stuck to her sweaty forehead. Even though it's raining outside, it's hot as hell in here.

"We got rid of it all like you asked—"

I cut her off with a sharp exhale.

"Not the big things, like the bed and stuff. The little stuff. Where is all the little stuff?"

Mom's face softens and for a moment, I'm terrified she's going to bring it up.

It.

We don't even have to have a name for that night, prom night. It's just ... *it.* That's all it deserves. Nothing more.

"They're in plastic bins, sealed airtight and stacked neatly in the rafters of the barn. Your dad even covered them with a tarp last year when we had that awful storm. They're perfectly safe." She set the cornbread on the counter, took off the mitt, and turned to look at me straight on. "Did you want me to help you load the bins into your car?"

"No," I say, because while I want them safe ... I do *not* want them anywhere near me. If I even *see* one of those bins, I'll open it and I'll start going through *his* letters and seeing *his* pictures and all the careful walls I've

spent four hundred and sixteen days building up will crumble to dust beneath my feet. "But thank you."

I turn and head back down the hall, ignoring the open door.

My bedroom no longer looks like my bedroom, and the carpet with all the familiar stains—the spot where *he* stepped on a tube of black paint, the melted fibers from that time I dropped a lit match, the frayed corner where Phoenix used to hide his cigarettes from my mom—is gone. The wood floors make it seem so different, the new paint colors help. But the window is the same, and it looks out at the same scenery, and I can barely even *stand* it.

I keep walking and find the den at the end of the hall, moving down two steps and into the sunken room that used to be the garage. You can hardly tell anymore —my dad did a good job with the remodel, but it sits a little lower and thankfully, seems to be a little cooler than the rest of the house.

In typical fashion, Mom's already fixed up the pull-out couch bed with blankets and pillows. I toss my duffel bag onto it, dig out some fresh clothes, and head for the shower.

I'm proud of myself for making it through the first fifteen minutes without crying.

Well, I haven't cried for … four hundred and twelve days so I guess that's not saying much. I just thought coming back here would stir it all up again … I just pray that I'm wrong about that.

━ ━ ━ ━ ━ ━ ━ ━ ━ ━ ━ ━ ━

Phoenix stops by while I'm in the shower.

I know he's here as soon as I set foot into the hallway, a towel wrapped around my naked body. Phoenix's voice is low and easy and sensual, like he's holding out a hand and inviting you to the bedroom even when he's just asking you out for lunch.

He was Codrick's best friend; he was mine.

Now, he's a stranger. We haven't talked since the funeral, not even once. Oh, he's tried. Texts and emails and messages on social media. He wasn't pushy, just persistent. At one point, I finally gave in and sent him a reply.

*Listen Phoenix, any strings I have that tie me to the past, they trip and tangle. They hang me and I start to choke. I'm sorry, but I just can't.*

That was six months ago; we haven't spoken since.

"Fuck," I curse, moving into the den and closing the door behind me.

My towel drops to the floor and I start digging around in my suitcase for something to wear, something nice. I know my dad likes to see me dressed up and I never do, not anymore. I used to be feminine and girly, always in pink with bright lipstick and big earrings and high heels.

I prefer sweats and loose tanks nowadays with boots or sneakers, anything that I can use to transition from a long day of class and studying and head straight to the gym. But my dad is sick and … if anything happens to him, I need to make sure that his last image of me makes him smile.

The door behind me opens and then Phoenix is just there, his hand tightening on the doorknob as I glance over my shoulder, wet strands of brunette hair sliding across my skin.

"Hey," I say, but I don't rush to cover up and Phoenix doesn't rush to leave.

I turn back to my bag and try to ignore the sudden tightening of my throat, the nervous twist in my belly. It's been six months since I last messaged him, but … four hundred and twelve days since I saw him.

*Holy shit. Holy shit. Holy shit.*

My hands are trembling as I dig through my clothes and snatch a pair of gray sweats and a white tank, yanking the two items on before I turn back around.

Phoenix is still there, but he's not looking at me anymore, his back to the room as he stands guard at the door.

"You can look now," I say, matching his pose with my arms crossed over my chest. He turns around slowly, carefully, almost like he's afraid to see me.

"Hello dere, Embry," he says slowly, his voice like shadows made sound, twisting around my body, making me shiver.

I cannot even *believe* that he's fucking here right now.

I'm in town for all of thirty minutes and he shows up?

I blame my mom.

"Phoenix," I say, glancing down at the carpet, at the chipped paint on my toenails. I used to get pedicures; my feet were always pretty. They're dry and chapped now, and the nails are ridiculously short. The only reason there's paint there at all is because I got this crazy idea in my head that I was going to go out with some friends and go dancing.

We ran into a group of guys and ended up partying.

I was having a good time, a great time.

Until I just wasn't anymore. I walked outside, got in a cab, and went back to the apartment. My roommates

were pissed, but they don't understand. They don't know what it's like to lose a soul mate.

Phoenix looks at me with his beautiful gray eyes, the color of a storm above the sea when the wind is howling fiercely and the waves are capped with white. His blonde hair is dyed a dark violet color, not long, not short, just this mussy in-between that reminds me of high school. He hasn't changed much since then.

Not that I expected him to.

Not having Codrick around, time seems to have slowed to a cruel crawl. A minute is a year to me. So even though it's 'only' been a year, to me it feels like centuries.

Still, nineteen year old Phoenix Benoit is even *more* beautiful than the eighteen year old version.

He leans against the wall with one shoulder and tries to hook a smile at me.

It's a beautiful smile, one that used to have girls weeping in the halls. But all it does is stir up memories like dust. My nostrils flare and sweat beads on my fore-head. *Fuck, when did he get all of those tattoos?*

There's one on his bicep that says *RIP Codrick.*

As I stare at Phoenix, standing there in black cargo shorts and a purple tank, it's all I can see.

RIP Codrick.

Rest in peace since you died in pain.

Bile rises in my throat and my vision blurs.

Maybe coming back here wasn't the right decision?

"What are you doing here?" I manage to choke out, turning back around and grabbing a brush, dragging it through my hair as the small step into the den creaks and I whirl back around to see Phoenix closing the distance between us.

"Your mom asked me to come over ..." he starts in that heavy Cajun accent of his, moving forward and making my entire body go cold. Phoenix walks around me and over to the shelf on the wall, searching through a row of books like he's got something specific in mind.

He tugs a paperback out and then holds it in one hand, exhaling as he turns to look at me, his gray eyes taking me in like it's been a century for him, too, like he doesn't recognize me at all.

"I missed you, Embry," he tells me, but I hate how husky and soft his voice sounds, and I don't know how to respond. Instead, I nod with my chin in his direction.

"You came in here for reading material?" I ask, and Phoenix smiles, that crooked little slash of mouth across a handsome face. My heart seizes in my chest and I close my eyes in an exaggerated blink. When I open them, Phoenix isn't smiling at me anymore.

"Your mom asked me to come in 'ere and grab dis for your dad. I … didn't know you were in here. I'm sorry. I shoulda knocked, me."

"Don't worry about it," I say, sweeping the brush through my hair a few more times and then hoping and praying the answer to my next question is *no*. "Are you going to the hospital with us?"

"Yeah, if dat's okay wit' you? Your dad and I got real close over da last year. I'd like to make sure he's okay." Phoenix taps the book against his palm and looks me over again, eyes taking in little details, like how corded my arm muscles are, how narrow my face. I used to have a round face with big cheeks. I was thin, but I was also soft. Now I'm hard and toned, dressed in gray instead of pink.

"You don't need my permission," I say, acting unusually harsh to the boy who's supposed to be my best friend. Was. Was my best friend.

Grabbing my duffel bag by the handle, I head back into the bathroom and close the door behind me—locking it.

And then I sink down to the floor and put my head in my hands.

Phoenix can't be my best friend anymore because … each memory we share of Codrick is a string that can trip, tangle, or hang me. And Phoenix and I … we share thousands.

Thousands and thousands of strings.

# PHOENIX

## CHAPTER TWO

Embry looks so damn different.

Like a ghost.

It's Codrick that died, but it's Embry who looks like a spirit.

Fuck.

I stand in da hallway outside da hospital room, waiting to be invited in by Noelie, Embry's mom. She welcomed me in earlier, but … even though I used ta feel like a member of da LeBlanc family … I don't no more. Not wit' Embry around anyway.

*Well, shit.*

Raking my fingers through my hair, I walk in a tight circle, exhaling sharply as I try to come to terms with Embry being in town again. All the dust I'd thought had settled since Codrick's death is floating around now, choking me.

"Hey Phoenix," one of the nurses says, pausing nearby. She's a little older than me—twenty-three, I think. We've fucked a couple o' times, but when I look at her ... I don't feel anything like I feel when I look at Embry.

God above knows there nobody like fuckin' Embry.

"Hey," I say, giving a tight-lipped smile that I hope says *leave me da hell alone.* I'm not in the mood for a quickie in the first floor bathroom. Not right now. No, the only thing I can think about right now is dat fucking girl—even if she looks at me like she wishes it were me that died.

Fuck, I wish every day that it was me that died.

To give Embry and Codrick a chance, a life together ... I'd have given up everything.

The nurse looks me up and down for a long moment and then walks away with a disappointed sounding sigh. I tuck my hands in my pockets and let out a sigh of my own, leaning against the window behind me and closing my eyes against the bright fluorescent glare of the hospital.

Seeing Embry makes me wonder who the fuck I've become and what the hell I'm doin'. I was supposed to go to college with her and Codrick, and instead ... I hung around this shit ass town and got myself into trouble.

"He's awake and wants to see you," Embry says, making me jump as I whirl around and find her standing

there starin' at me, an apparition of a time past, a beautiful nightmare come back to haunt me.

She isn't dark and brooding right now, dressed in gray sweats and a scowl, with muscles as hard as my own. She's dressed up to see her father and ... now I'm thinking about Codrick and how much he loved her, about the three of us swimming in the lake, taking weekend trips to New Orleans, lying in bed and talkin' about our dreams of the future

And damn it if those dreams haven't been shattered to shit.

"You okay?" Embry asks, narrowing her brown eyes. Just that simple motion transforms her from the gorgeous, carefree teenager I knew to the skeptical, broken woman she's become.

The bouncy curls, pink lipstick, and big gold earrings don't change any o' dat.

"Yeah, I'm fine, me," I say with a sharp exhale, shaking out my hands and trying not to think of all the things I gotta do later. All the people I gotta meet up with. People who don't exactly have my best interests in mind, no.

I got real jumpy since Embry left, getting mixed up in all sorts of shit.

I barely sleep at night now.

"I'm fine," I repeat when she raises her brows and steps back, welcoming me into Devin's hospital room. I've been helping out da family and bringing Devin 'ere for all sorts of tests these last few weeks. And yet he still had the heart attack. It ain't right, no, for a man this good to be struck so low.

The normally strong, unflappable patriarch of the LeBlanc family looks as much like a ghost as his daughter—just in a different way.

And I'm a superstitious motherfucker, me.

Dere are spirits all over da damn place.

Exhaling, I move over to the side of the bed and place a hoodoo charm in Devin's big hand. He mighta lost a lot of weight, but no matter how far his bones stick outta his face, he's got big hands and big feet, a proud man who don't let nothin' bother him.

"Phoenix," he says, his voice rough and strangled, not at all like I'm used to. For me, Devin is da father I never really had. He was da big, gentle male hand to ruffle my hair and teach me to throw and hug me when I cried.

My own dad, he wasn't a monster so much as he was a whirlwind, always caught up in somethin'. The same somethin' I told myself I'd never get involved in. That same somethin' that's eating me alive from da inside out.

"You feelin' better, *mon Père*?" I ask with a grin, noticing the older man clutching the paperback book against his chest. I'm always bringin' him books now since he's stuck inside all da damn time. This here's a man who's used to working with his hands, who's always outside doing somethin'.

Being laid flat is not in Devin's wheelhouse.

"I feel alright. I'd like to get out of this damn bed though," he says, his accent so much different than mine. I have backwoods and bayou and *L'Acadiane* scrawled all over me. Devin is from Louisiana, too, but farther north. I can't remember where just now. Don't matter anyhow. Even if we talk different, we still family.

*Well* ...

Glancing over my shoulder, I find Embry staring at me with big, brown eyes, shadowed in pink with golden glitter sparkles. It used to make her eyes look like they were shining. But now? No, it just looks like a joke, yeah.

The whole reason I was welcome into the LeBlanc family in da first place was because o' her. Embry. Fuck. My best friend, my longest friend except for Codrick. He always used to joke that it coulda been either one of us that she fell in love with. That we were two minutes apart from being her man.

He was her first, friended her first … but I never minded.

Now, though? Now she's lookin' at me like she wishes I was anywhere but here wit' her and her family.

"Embry," Devin calls out, waving his youngest daughter around to the other side of the bed. She takes his hand, but the way she looks at him … it's like he's already dead. "It's good to have you home, honey."

Embry's mouth tightens when she smiles and not a lick o' dat false joy even reaches her eyes. No, she really does look like a ghost.

"Thanks, Dad," she says, but she doesn't agree with his words.

No, because she don't agree with him.

Not one bit.

"You're smoking?" Embry asks me, her heels loud in the shadows as I crouch on the edge of hospital property and take a drag on a cigarette. "I thought you quit?"

"Yeah, well," I say as I blow white smoke into the navy darkness and listen to the distant whisper of cicadas. So loud at night, they are. Even here in da city where humans took over everything. It's why I still live

where I live, because I like it out dere in the middle o' nowhere.

No city lights, no traffic noises, no people.

But even I get lonely sometimes, me.

I continue smoking my cigarette, but I don't bother to explain.

We both know why I started smoking again.

"My dad was more excited to see you than me," Embry says, but she doesn't sound upset. Actually, she sounds a bit happy about it? I flick my gaze her direction, the bright burn of my cigarette lighting up the tattoos on my fingers. I have hundreds of 'em now. Hundreds. Used to be just a mark here and dere, but … things have changed since Codrick died.

Vices—like smoking—aren't just annoying habits to be broken. Oh no, they be as important as air in da lungs, food in da belly, a warm body in da bed … I sigh.

The feel of the needle against my skin is one of the few things that makes me feel awake, alive. And since the only legitimate job I work is at a tattoo shop, I have plenty of chances to go under dat needle.

"Nah, he just not used to dat pretty face o' yours anymore," I grumble around the cigarette, leaning forward and pulling out a small object from my back pocket. Embry stands near me, the sweet fragrance of her scent wafting in the dark air like a drug. I want to follow it close, wrap my arms around her and hold her tight. If I could, I'd let her take a knife to my heart, sacrifice me so Codrick could live.

I bet she wishes for dat, too.

"Here," I tell her as I pass over a small key. It's the house key she left behind when she left for college. Her mom gave it to me, but I want to give it back. I want her to stay. Even though I know it's temporary, I want— even for just a moment—things to be like they used to be.

What I already done though, is take Codrick's house key off the ring. Since Embry left town, I've been carrying the ring around with me, all the old keys still on it. But I worried that if I gave it back to her like that, she'd break.

Fuck, Embry was always one of the strongest people I've ever known.

But now ... she looks like glass.

"Thanks," she says, studying the piece of metal in her palm. "I'm gonna head home and get some sleep. It was a long drive."

"I can only imagine," I say as she hesitates for a moment, and then starts walking away. Without thinking, I reach out and put my hand on her arm.

"I missed you, ya know," I say, my voice low and gruff.

My fingers on Embry's arm feel like they're catching fire, heat blooming underneath my fingertips and racing up my arm.

"I …" she starts, but then she pulls away and casts a look over her shoulder that I can't read in the dark. "Thanks."

Embry turns on her heel, her shoes echoing loudly around the parking lot.

New Orleans is a dangerous, dangerous place, so I watch her go, climb in her car, slam the door.

And then I get on my bike and I follow her home, just to make sure she gets there alright.

If I sit outside for a while and watch the glow from the windows, well that's just a selfish act for little ol' me.

# EMBRY

## CHAPTER THREE

My dreams are thick with grief and blood, and I wake up sweating, missing Codrick and reliving those awful moments all over again, those first few seconds of seeing the car, crumpled and ruined, the first few seconds of seeing his hand, the roses, the blood …

Racing into the bathroom, I throw up three times and end up crawling into a hot shower to lie on my side.

But I don't cry.

All that pain inside of me and I don't shed a single tear.

Back at school, only two of my friends know and even then, I wish I'd never told them.

*It's been a year, get over it. It's time to start dating again.*

*Don't be whiny, Embry. Nobody likes a whiner.*

But they don't understand—I'm not whining.

I'm fucking grieving.

And real grief, real love, it doesn't have a timer on it, some schedule you put your emotions on until they run their course. I know for a fact that I'll have to live the rest of my life loving Codrick, missing Codrick, regretting everything that went down that night.

It's like I lost a limb, a piece of me I can never get back.

And there's no prosthetic for a cold, dead, and broken heart.

Climbing back into bed, I try to go to sleep and find out quite quickly that that's never going to happen. Not this night. My first night at home.

I'm not surprised.

Slipping into a hoodie—one of Phoenix's old ones, actually—I head outside and stand on the porch in the freezing air. January in Donaldsonville is *cold*. A quick glance at my phone shows it's literally below freezing out.

Fuck, I want to go home.

And this, it isn't home anymore.

Home is where the heart is, and my heart is dead.

He died all alone, in the rain, in the dark, the boy that called me baby girl.

Putting my hands on my face, I drag them down my skin and stifle a scream. I don't want my mom and sisters to come running. With Dad in the hospital, they're all on edge. The last thing I need to do is give *mom* a heart attack, too.

Stepping back inside, I grab my keys off a hook near the door and climb into my car, knowing that I'm going to regret this as soon as I get on the road and start driving.

I don't call to announce myself, instead driving forty-five minutes into the swamp to Phoenix's house.

Honestly, at this point, we're virtually strangers, but … here I am at home and there's nobody else in the world—not even Codrick's mother—that understands the true pain of his loss. Selfishly, I believe that I'm hurting most, but in the dark shadows inside my chest, I know that Phoenix hurts the same as I do.

He lost his best friend, basically his brother, on a dark and stormy night.

And then he lost me, too.

Based on my mom and sisters' gossip, I know Phoenix still lives in the same shit trailer in the middle of the fucking bayou. Why he hasn't left is beyond me. Maybe, the way Rick's death sent me running, it trapped Phoenix in place like the thick gooey, mud I step in when I climb out of the car.

His bike is in the driveway. Well, it's not the bike I remember him driving in high school, but I know he wrecked that one, so it's no surprise to see a new one

there. The only thing is … it looks awfully shiny and expensive.

Running my fingers over the chrome handlebars, I move up toward the sagging porch and the front door with the dartboard still hanging crookedly from it. There were evenings we all sat out here in lawn chairs and lazily tossed darts at the door, sipping beer from Solo cups and shooting the breeze.

Those days are long gone, dead and buried.

Swallowing hard, I knock on the door and feel my heart thundering in my chest.

The old wood swings inward and then there's Phoenix standing there with a cigarette hanging out of his mouth, shirtless and beautiful and draped in ink. His holey jeans hang low on his hips and his smell … I can almost *taste* that musky masculine odor on my tongue.

"Hey," I whisper, my voice husky and shredded. I haven't been with a man since Codrick and … I think my hormones are going nuts, electrical impulses shooting through me like lightning bolts.

"Embry," Phoenix chokes out, his eyes, the color of thunderclouds, bulging out of his head. "What are you doing here?!" He sounds … flustered. I guess he would be, considering it's almost three in the morning. Shit, I didn't even think about what I was doing. He could've been asleep or out partying or …

"Something wrong?" a feminine voice asks from behind Phoenix.

Footsteps pad across the old, creaky floors and then two pale arms slide around the Cajun's tanned chest.

As soon as I see her touch him, something snaps inside of me.

I feel sick.

"Sorry," I say, backing up suddenly.

Even though I've been here a million times before, somehow I forget that the step is broken and there's nothing but a hole on the left side. My foot falls through it and I pinwheel backward, arms flailing.

Phoenix lunges forward, dislodging his feminine guest—who smells like peaches and vanilla, ugh—and grabs me around the waist before I can fall on my ass in the mud, tugging me forward and against the scalding warmth of his chest.

"*Merde,* baby girl," he mutters and then we both freeze.

We freeze and everything around us ceases to exist —the swamp, the mud, the freezing rain that's just started to fall, the girl whimpering in the background.

"What?" I whisper, because we both know what he just said.

Just like he did at the funeral.

*Baby Girl.*

Baby Girl.

The words that trigger me more than anything … Baby fucking Girl.

Jerking away from Phoenix's arms, I stumble and fall from the porch, knees sinking into the mud. My breath chokes out of me as I scramble up, Phoenix's fingers curling around my arm and jerking me back around to face him.

Rain plasters his hair to his forehead, the same way it did to Codrick's when he was lying dead on the road.

"'Ey girl, listen to me!" Phoenix is shouting, but I try to pull away from him anyway. He's strong, but so am I. I've spent the last four hundred and twelve days working out every spare second I can get.

We end up tussling, falling into the mud and rolling around until Phoenix literally pins me to the ground.

"I'm not letting you drive away like this!" he screams, my muscles straining as I struggle to pull my arms from his grip. "No way, no how am I letting you go, me." Phoenix yanks me to my feet and picks me up, tossing me over his shoulder.

I kick and flail, pushing myself off his muscular back and *biting* him.

That's how pissed off I am.

Except ... his skin tastes good, musky and sweet at the same time. There's a hint of that mint soap my mother makes, a bit of sweat, the icy drench of rain.

Phoenix growls beneath me, a rumbling beast of hard muscles and tattoos, and then sets me down on the porch.

His girlfriend is still standing there in an oversized pink t-shirt, big blonde curls frothing around her face.

As soon as Phoenix lets go of me, I shove past her and she makes a sound as I smear mud across her perfect arm. Heading through the narrow living room, I push open the door on the far end that used to lead outside and to the *outhouse*.

Freshman year of high school, my dad came out here and built the Benoits a bathroom with a toilet, sink, tub, *and* shower. Hell, it's nicer than the one at our own house. My dad never does anything in half-measures. He takes fucking pride in his work.

I slip inside and slam the door behind me, locking it and stripping off all my muddy clothes. Rinsing them as best I can in the sink, I turn on the hot heat of the shower and climb under it, sitting down on the ground with my arms wrapped around my knees.

A few minutes later, after the bathroom is shrouded with steam, I stand back up and open the little window on my left, letting the cool night suck some of the heat from the air. It feels so good to stand like that, hot water scalding my flesh while freezing cold air fills my lungs.

"You hit like a tank and bite like a snake," Phoenix mumbles, making me jump. I jerk back part of the curtain to glare at him, standing there with a black tank on, like he's got something to hide underneath it. "I don' remember sweet Embry being so damn feisty." He pauses and looks me straight in the face, making me acutely aware of my nakedness. My nipples harden to points and I swallow the sudden lump in my throat.

I haven't seen the man in four hundred and twelve days.

He has a girlfriend standing right outside this door.

And …

"What the fuck are you doing in here? I locked the door for a reason. Get *out*."

"First off, you know I can pick a lock like nobody else, me. Second, this might be the only moment I get to talk some sense into you. You trapped in dere unless you want me to see you naked."

Phoenix smiles, but the expression is tight, haunted, far away.

He's so fucked-up.

And here I am, twice as fucked and driving out to his house in the middle of the goddamn night. I must've developed sleepwalking tendencies in the past twenty-four hours because I have no goddamn clue why I'd even think something like this was okay.

"I'm not lettin' you drive home in this mess."

"You think you can *let* or not *let* me do anything?" I snap, curling my fingers in the shower curtain. Phoenix just stares at me with his beautiful gray eyes, the color of the gulf on a cloudy day, when the sun shines through them just right. Just fucking right. His tight smile slowly curls into a frown. "People drive all the time in the rain and they don't die," I say.

They don't die.

But he did.

Codrick died.

He swerved and his car flipped and he died.

But I'm not afraid to drive in the rain.

Because I'm not afraid to die.

"Just stay the night, you," he says, shaking his head and lifting up a pile of folded clothes in his hands. "You can have the bed and I'll sleep on the couch."

"Where's your girlfriend going to sleep?" I ask as Phoenix sighs and shakes his head, setting the clothes on the counter so he can rake his fingers through his violet hair. It's this dark but saturated color that suits his gray eyes as well as his skin, tanned and weathered from the sun. He always used to say he was part Mama, but all Papa.

"She ain't my girlfriend, that girl."

"Whatever," I say, throwing the curtain back into place and wondering if there's something wrong with me because I really want that girl to leave. I don't want her here. And I *really* don't want to spend the night in Phoenix's bed knowing she's fucking him on the couch. That's disgusting.

Grabbing a bar of soap from the shelf, I hold it in my hand and then lift it to my nose.

This is most *definitely* one of Mom's.

Goat milk, mint, and lavender. She sells bars of soap at the flea market every weekend, has for years. I heft it in my hand and then give it another sniff. It smells like Phoenix's skin tasted.

Lathering up my body, I get myself as clean as I can and climb out of the shower.

Phoenix is gone, thankfully, so I grab a delightfully fluffy towel from the stack of clothes, dry off, and slip into a giant t-shirt and sweats so baggy, they slide down my hips when I walk.

"Can I get a plastic bag for my clothes?" I ask when I open the door, towel drying my hair and finding myself face-to-face with the woman that smells like peaches.

"Yeah, you can," she says, thrusting an empty grocery bag out in her fist and shaking it at me. "Now put your stuff in it and *go*. I would leave, but you know, *he* drove me out here on his motorcycle and I don't have a car." The girl narrows pale blue eyes at me in triumph and tosses a smirk my way. "Plus, I really just don't feel comfortable with you here, wearing his clothes, when I'm the one that's fucking him."

"He goes through girls like old socks," I say, giving her a mean sort of look that I really don't feel all that deep inside of me. Phoenix is the one that picked this woman up and brought her all the way out here for sex. Instead of treating this girl like there's something wrong with her, I should be emphasizing that I think there's something wrong with him.

Only ... I don't.

If I could fuck away the pain, I would, too.

I'd do it and I wouldn't look back. Those few moments of pleasure probably offer a sort of reprieve, a vacation away from the nightmare of the mind. Masturbation helps me *a little*, but maybe if I had a partner, I could pretend he was Codrick? I could pretend that I didn't see the love of my life bleeding to death on the side of the road with flowers for me clutched in his dead hand.

Swallowing hard, I turn back and shove my clothes in the plastic bag while Peaches and Cream glares and glares and fucking glares at me.

"We've been friends forever," I snap at her, wondering where the fuck Phoenix is when he should be standing here dealing with this crap. His house is literally one room with an attached bedroom and this bathroom. There aren't a lot of places to hide.

"Sorry girls," he says, coming out of the bedroom. He looked liked he'd cleaned up pretty damn good before he peeped on me in the bathroom, but now that I'm looking closer, I see there's mud in his hair and streaked along the side of his face. "Just changin' da sheets and grabbing some bedding."

"I'm not staying here," I repeat as I dig through my clothes for my keys.

They're not there.

*That motherfucker ....*

"Where are my keys, Phoenix?" I ask, whipping around to glare over Peaches and Cream's bare shoulder. Her big baggy pink tee has slid down, flashing tattoos on her perfect skin. I haven't gotten any ink. I imagine that if I did, I'd remember that moment forever. Even if I tried to forget, it'd be right there on my skin, stirring up new memories.

My power lies in knowing how to forget.

"You ain't driving in that rain, you!" he shouts, tossing the blankets and pillows in his arms onto the couch. Phoenix throws out one tattooed arm toward the front windows for emphasis and the house rattles and shakes in the wind, as if warning me against driving in the dark and the wet.

Shoving my clothes in the plastic bag, I tie the top up and push past Peaches, striding up to Phoenix and leaning forward, thrusting my hand into the pocket of his sweats. First one and then the other.

I don't find my keys, but I do feel that strange hot warmth in my chest bubbling, frothing, like boiling water sloshing around behind my ribs.

Oh.

Oh, oh, fuck.

Stumbling back from Phoenix, I chuck the heavy bag of wet clothes against the wall near the front door and sit on the couch. It's not the same one he's always had, the one his Dad brought home with a *FREE* sign still taped to it.

This couch is leather, like *real* leather and comfortable as hell.

As I sit there … I realize that the shitty little swamp shack where Phoenix has lived his whole life has gotten a serious upgrade. The coffee table and chairs are new, there are framed paintings on the wall, and when I glance over my shoulder at the kitchenette, I see brand-new appliances and a small island with a stone top.

What. The. Fuck.

"This place sure has changed," I say as Phoenix opens the fridge and brings me a cool bottle of beer, placing it in my hand. Our fingers brush together and something strange happens in my chest, this twisting, tightening sensation that makes me feel like I might throw up.

*What is wrong with me right now?*

"I'm in charge here now, me," Phoenix says, taking a seat in the chair on my left. The girl comes over in her pink shirt, a beer wrapped in her long fingers and manicured nails. She tries to sit on Phoenix's lap, but he holds up a palm. "No, sorry dere girl, but I got a guest now."

"So I can't sit on your lap?" she asks, flicking her gaze to me like she'd tear the flesh from my bones with her nails if she could. I try not to judge her. Back in the day, if a woman had shown up at Codrick's house while I was … but no, this girl is nothing like I was. And her relationship with Phoenix is *nothing* like what I had with Codrick.

What she's glaring at me over … it's a joke.

"Sit down and have a beer?" he suggests, gesturing at the other chair with an inked hand. The girl makes a sound in her throat, something seriously akin to a growl and then sloshes the beer in her bottle all over my childhood friend.

*"Pouyaille!"* he curses under his breath, standing up and dripping as Peaches marches into his bedroom and slams the door.

I look at him, wondering if I should apologize for showing up like a crazy person in the middle of the night but ... no. He brings these girls home to use them for sex? He can put up with the fallout.

"'Ey, where you goin', girl?" Phoenix calls out as he tears his wet tank over his head and bares his gorgeous chest and abs again. I can hardly *look* at him like that. It's ... he's almost impossibly beautiful. I remember him being pretty, always. But he's grown into a ridiculously handsome man.

"My friend is coming to pick me up," Peaches spits back at him, storming out of Phoenix's bedroom in a white floral print dress with tall red heels. She storms to the front door, opens it, and then glares back at Phoenix. "Lose my number, asshole."

She steps outside and slams the door behind her.

Her exit is a little less dramatic than I think she probably wanted because both Phoenix and I can hear her griping to someone over the phone.

"You'll let her drive away in the dark and not me?" I ask as he mops up some of the beer with his shirt, looking down at me with eyes that draw me in, that make my breath catch in my throat, my heart flip-flop in my chest.

"She ain't you, Embry," he says, looking at me for a long, long moment, his violet hair shimmering in the lamplight. Lamps. Hah. Phoenix's dad never had lamps. The two bare bulbs that used to shimmer from the ceiling—one in the kitchen and one in the living room—are gone. When I glance up ... I see recessed lighting. "She ain't you," Phoenix mutters, moving around the back of the couch and into the hallway. I see him open two doors that used to lead to a very narrow closet ... and find myself gaping when I see a shiny new washer and dryer.

I want to ask where the fuck he got all of this stuff, but I bite my tongue.

We're not there yet.

Right now, we're dancing this strange waltz of strangers and friends. I can't decide which of the two I want to be. No, no, I want to stay strangers.

Swallowing hard, I shake my head and suck down half of my beer, sending a text to both my sisters and my mom before they wake up and find me missing.

"You shouldn't have taken my keys," I say as Phoenix washes up and comes back into the living room ... still shirtless. Damn it. "We don't know each other like that anymore."

He laughs at me then, shaking his head and wiping off his chair with a washrag before he takes a seat again.

"You can't un-know somebody, Embry, even if you wish you could," Phoenix says, his silver eyes glazing over slightly as he glances to the left and stares at the old cast-iron stove. It looks clean, well-taken care of, and there's a fire crackling away inside.

God, this place has changed so much since Phoenix's dad Thibaut—pronounced *T-boe*—passed away.

So so much.

For the better, it seems.

It's actually kind of cozy in here now.

"You …" I start, sipping my beer and finding my words all twisted inside my head. I don't know what to say. I want to ask if he'd un-know Codrick if he could, if he'd wipe all those memories away like they'd never been. As much as I'm hurting inside, I'd rather die than lose a single second of time I spent with my soul mate. "Thanks for the beer," I say instead, changing the subject. "I should get to bed. I'll probably be gone before you wake up."

"Wait," Phoenix says, reaching out and snatching my wrist. His fingers are ridiculously warm against my skin. "Why did you come out here anyway? Dere gotta be a reason you drove all the way into the swamp just to see me, yeah?"

Looking down at him, I have no idea what to say.

Why *did* I come out here? Was it because I wanted to talk about Codrick?

No.

I choose to forget him at the same time I won't let go. It's a strange paradox, clinging tight to the past while sprinting as fast as I can into the future.

"I don't know," I say as I yank my wrist from his grasp, backing up to put some space between us. Heading around the back of the sofa, I deposit my empty beer bottle on the fancy new kitchen island, and then head into Phoenix's bedroom.

With the door closed behind me, I curl up on his bed and breathe in his smell.

I refuse to admit that I find it comforting.

# PHOENIX

## CHAPTER FOUR

It's agony knowing that Embry is sleeping in my bed, but seemingly doesn't want anything to do with me either.

Fuck.

But she came all the way out here for a reason, right? There had to be *some* reason she drove almost an hour into the swamp at three in the fuckin' morning?

Raking my fingers through my hair, I fall back into the pillows and close my eyes. I don't think I'm gonna be able to sleep, no. Not with memories of Embry and Codrick swirling through my head, making my heart hurt like nothin' else.

*"I believe people can have more than one soul mate,"* Codrick says, his dark hair shining as he glances back at me. I know he sees the way I look at Embry, but it don' matter. Not wit' us. No, he knows I'd rather die than come between him and his girl. "Don't you?"

I wake up before I can hear my own answer, a loud knocking at the door alerting me to the bright sunshine streaming through the window, the alarm on my phone ringing from the surface of the coffee table.

Shit.

I almost slept right through it.

Throwing my feet on the floor, I move quickly to the front door, checking out the window before I open it.

Fuck. It's Roch.

I was hopin' Embry was still gonna be here, curled up in my bed and sleeping soundly, but now that I know who's at my door, I pray that she be gone already, back to her Mama's cozy house for breakfast.

Taking a deep breath, I grab the gun from the small side table near the door and shove it into the waistband of my jeans, the pressure of the weapon against my spine a comforting sensation.

Yanking the door open, I see Roch's scowl before his fist flies out and hits me right in da face.

Blood sprays out as I stumble back and two other men come from around the corner of the house. As I move away from them, I catch a quick glimpse out at the driveway and see that Embry's car is gone.

*Thank fuck.*

"Where the hell is she?" Roch asks as his two friends join him and step up close on either side. I figure they be tryin' to pin me in, but I'm not stupid. My Dad might not've been the world's greatest parent, but he taught me some tricks, that's for sure.

I won't let myself get boxed in.

"Where da hell is who?" I growl back, shoving my fist across the bottom half of my face. Blood smears over the inked designs on my knuckles as I look at a man that nobody in their right mind would wanna piss off.

"Eliette," he snaps, taking a menacing step toward me.

The man is big and thick all over with tree trunks for arms and legs, and a head that's the shape of a block. I look at him and I wonder how he'd ever pick up girls if not for his reputation as rich, dangerous, and connected.

No, no girls would not flock to this man's bed if he was a regular joe.

"She left last night," I snap, throwing out a hand to indicate the couch with its pile of blankets and pillows. "A friend o' mine stopped by and Eliette didn't want to stay and chat, if you know what I mean."

The edges of Roch's lips curl up in a snarl and he makes his way toward me with a growl churning in his throat, like some sort of animal.

"My *sister* was here last night, and now she's missing. That doesn't paint a very pretty picture of you, now does it?"

His sister?

Fuck.

Fuck, fuck, fuck.

I wasn't thinking last night when I left Embry's house.

Seeing her again twisted me up inside, and I found myself at da club. I didn't know who I was picking up. Shit, I just picked the first girl with a pretty smile and brought her home. We didn't even have sex—Embry showed up before we'd gotten past a few beers and some foreplay.

"She said a friend was picking her up," I say as I think about the driving rain and wonder if my callous attitude last night got a girl struck dead. Did her friend crash the car and kill them both? There's a hollow feeling in my chest as I look into Roch's eyes. Not only am I worried about dat girl and her friend now, but dis guy here? He looks at me like he thinks I done somethin' to her.

I can't have a guy like this thinkin' I hurt his sister.

That wouldn't end well for little ol' me.

"What kind of car was the friend driving?" Roch asks me, his dark hair hanging to his shoulders in loose waves, his face stubbled and rough but more like just forgot to shave and not at all like he's trying to be suave.

"I didn't see a car, me," I say, reaching around to scratch my lower back. The men with Roch stiffen up, but they don't pull their guns. Good. Now if I really do have to shoot them, I just bought myself an extra second or two to pull my pistol. "But I know it was gettin' close to four when I heard 'em peel out of here."

Roch looks at me long and hard and then scowls.

"Just show up on time tonight, fuckin' coon-ass."

I grit my teeth as he turns to go, waving his friends along with him.

"*Pic kee toi*," I curse under my breath slamming the door hard enough to rattle all da crap on the wall shelves. *Fuck you* is what dat means. Motherfucker had worse comin' his way, too.

As if I were stupid *or* heartless enough to hurt some poor girl.

Now I just gotta wonder if she got in an accident … or if somebody else *was* that heartless or cruel.

And if I gonna find myself fuckin' blamed for it.

Could be in big trouble, me.

■ ▪ ■ ▪ ■ ▪ ■ ▪ ■ ▪ ■ ▪ ■

A few hours later, I get myself all cleaned up and head over to the LeBlancs.

Baby Girl

I tell myself I'm checkin' on Noelie, makin' sure she's alright, seein' if she needs anything done around the house or the yard … But really, I know I'm going over there to see Embry.

Pounding up the steps, I reach for my key, realize I already gave it back, and then raise my fist to knock.

Embry's sister opens the door with a wide grin, her brown hair curled around her shoulders, her makeup as flawless as always. She's got a baby on one hip, but the way she bats her eyes reminds me that she's recently divorced. Not that I'm interested, but looks like she might be.

"We heard your bike," she tells me, her Southern accent as sweet and perky as her little sister's used to be. Ah, shoot, that *fillette* used to be the cutest Southern belle—well-mannered and peppy, feminine and strong, a girl who don' take no shit but don' give it unless deserved.

She talks like a New Yorker now, dat girl.

"It's dat loud, huh?" I ask as I scuff my boots against the welcome mat and look up to see Embry's mother smiling at me from the kitchen.

"You're just in time for lunch," Noelie says as she jerks her head in the direction of the hallway. "Go down there and grab Embry for me, will you? She's been sitting in the dark listening to her headphones all darn day."

"Yes, ma'am," I say with a nod of my chin and a small grin.

Heading across the new hardwood floors that I helped Devin install, I move down the hallway and past Embry's old bedroom. The urge to reach for that knob, push it open and see Rick and Embry cuddling on da bed, waiting for me ...

My heart contracts painfully and I push myself forward, pausing outside the door to the den and wondering if I should knock. Because oh, dat was a serious treat last time. But no, dat was an accident. If I peep on dis girl on purpose, that's just sick.

Knocking a few times, I get no answer and figure she must be listening to her music still.

I let myself in and move over to the edge of the bed, sitting down on the side of the mattress. Embry's back is to me, her body curled in a tight, little fetal position.

"You awake?" I ask, my voice echoing in the shadows of the den. The blinds are down, light leaking between them, making the dust motes dance like fireflies. When I was a kid, there were fireflies fuckin' everywhere in the swamp.

There ain't a lot left now.

I wait for a minute, listening to the music leaking out of Embry's headphones, turning toward her and putting my knee up on the bed. Reaching over, I tug on one of the earbuds and pull it free.

"Hey."

She jumps like she's been punched, sitting up and looking at me with wide, glassy eyes, like she has no idea where she is or what's going on.

That's how she looked that night, when she climbed off my motorcycle and stumbled over to Codrick's body. Like a ghost. A zombie. A broken spirit with no reason to keep living.

"What do you want?" Embry asks, swallowing several times, like she's trying to choke back tears. She cried so much then, and I just held her and held her. But then … she packed up those bags and left, dropped me in the bloody aftermath of Codrick's death.

I never faulted her for dat.

I shoulda got outta here, too.

I shoulda ran and never looked back.

"Your mom made lunch," I say, but the look she gives me says she doesn't give a *fuck* about food. "You gonna spend your whole visit locked up in dis room here?" I gesture at the cramped old den, deer and gator heads on the wall, dust coating the old shelves with sticks and rocks and bones, treasures from the swamp.

"What's the point of coming to see your family if you won't have gumbo wit' dem?"

"Get out, Phoenix," she says, her voice as brittle as old wood, ready to snap at a single hard footfall. Looking at her, I feel as broken, as wrecked now as I did that fateful day. Neither of us has moved on, not even close.

Shit. *Moving on* is out of our league, too. We still grieving, me and dis girl.

"You want to go see him?" I ask, and I don't have to say who *he* is.

We both know exactly who I'm talking about.

"See him?" she replies, tearing out her second earbud and giving me a look like I'm stupid. "We can't go see Codrick, Phoenix. He's fucking *dead*. An expensive plot of land and a crypt with his family's last name on it … no thanks. I'd rather stay here." Embry stops, her nostrils flaring, her eyes closing like the rush of emotion is too much to bear.

"Okay," I say, because I don't wanna spook her and I don't know shit about anything. If I were an expert on grief, I wouldn't think about how much better things would be if Codrick were alive every single fucking day.

I move to stand up and Embry makes a small sound in her throat, giving me pause.

"I'm writing a paper about grief," she says, surprising me. "Would it be okay if I interviewed you?"

70

Standing there, looking down at Embry, I just want to put my hands on either side of her face, run my thumb over her lower lip. I want to lean down and feel her breath feather against my mouth …

"Yeah, okay," I say, sitting back down on the end of the bed.

She looks at me for a long moment and then turns away, rolling onto her belly and grabbing her bag from the floor. She drags it onto the mattress, sits up, and digs through it until she finds her computer.

Flipping the top open, she wiggles into a more comfortable position as I stare at her, tendrils of dark hair falling forward across her face. *Fuck, she's so beautiful,* I think, my heart twisting and aching fiercely inside my chest. *I shoulda chased after her when Codrick died.*

But she didn't want me, and I was hurting too much to fight her. She said she didn't want me around no more, and I listened.

Glancing sharply away, I try not to see the ghost of Codrick sitting in the chair across the room, frowning at the two of us.

*"Ask her out, man. She won't wait around forever, you know?"*

*"Brother, I must be goin' crazy to be talkin' to you. Codrick, you're already dead, you. What do you care what happens between me and your girl?"*

*"I loved you two more than I loved anyone else. You know that, right?"*

Tearing my gaze away from Rick's ghost, I refocus on Embry. She's staring at me like she can somehow sense what I'm up to over here, fucking goin' loony inside my own head, talkin' to dead men. I'd be better off chattin' up the gators that hang out in my backyard, mouths open as dey sun demselves.

"I'm going to ask you a series of questions," she says, exhaling sharply and turning the computer around so I can see that it's recording a video of our conversation. "Are you okay with me recording this for my research paper?"

"Yeah, I'm okay wit' dat," I say, and Embry nods, taking a deep breath and reaching for a case on the side table next to the bed. She flips it open, grabs a pair of thick rimmed glasses and slips them on her face. Back in da day, I wouldn't see her in glasses unless I snuck through her window so early in da morning that she was still asleep. She was religious about putting her contacts in.

I remember one time when we were camping, Codrick and I woke up and she was gone. We thought a cottonmouth or a gator got her when she went out to pee and we panicked. We were crazy men, tearing apart da

forest, screaming at the top of our lungs … Dat girl was over at the edge of the lake putting her contacts in.

Fuck, those days … I miss 'em.

Embry grabs a binder from her bag and then takes out a sheet of paper with handwritten questions on it. Her voice, when she speaks, is robotic and dry, like the spirit been bled out of her and it never comin' back.

"First question," she begins, choking slightly as she stares through the black rimmed glasses at the paper. "Tell me your name."

I cock a brow, but Embry flicks her gaze up to mine and purses her lips.

"Phoenix Avit Benoit," I say and she nods.

"And is there a specific incident you want to talk about with me today? Regarding grief?"

"Uh," I start, but she sighs and drops the paper into her lap.

"Just pretend you don't know me," she says, looking hard at my face, "or that I don't know anything about Codrick." Her voice catches on his name and I see her hands tremble. But she don't cry. Maybe she cried herself all out of tears this past year? "Can you do that for me?"

"I can do that," I say as she sighs and starts over again, asking my name, repeating the second question in that monotone voice.

"My best friend, basically my *brudder*," I mumble and feel my lids get heavy with grief. *Shit. I wanna punch something. Good thing I get to punch the hell out of some asshole tonight.* "He died in a car accident on the night of our senior prom."

Embry makes another sound in her throat, but when I look back up at her, her face is blank and empty.

"How long ago was that?" she asks and I feel my shoulders get tight.

"Four hundred and seventeen days," I whisper, because why the hell wouldn't I be counting them? Each one seems harder than the last—especially since Embry left. Looking at her now, I realize it ain't only Codrick that made my heart hurt so bad.

"And ..." she starts, her hands trembling even harder.

I want nothing more than to reach out and take hold of them in mine.

"And ..." She tries to speak again, but the words don't seem to want to come out. "*And ...*"

"Each moment since then's been a chore," I whisper, leaning forward and doing exactly what I want to do, taking Embry's hands in mine and rubbing a thumb over her knuckles. The motion stirs up all this heat and emotion between us, making my muscles feel tight, my tongue swollen, my throat dry. "Each day I wake up and

wonder why. Why it was him and not me. Why he had to die that night. If there was something I coulda done to change it."

"You … can …" Embry starts as I scoot further onto the bed. "Have you found a … has there been a method … How have you found ways to cope?"

"Cope?" I ask, taking the paper away from those trembling hands. "Fuck, you know I haven't found a way to cope, Embry. I'm a mess, me."

"I … I don't want to do this anymore," she says, taking her hands away from mine and snapping the lid of her laptop closed on the paper. "Never mind. This was stupid."

"You don't have to run away," I whisper, wishing she'd just let go. She looks wound all the way up, and it's killing me to see it. Two days she been back and it's stressing *me* out.

"Run away?" she asks, turning her melancholy to anger, eyes widening in righteous indignation. "I'm not running away. I'm trying not to fall apart!" She pushes away from me and stands up, raking long fingers through her gorgeous dark hair.

Fuck, I want to be runnin' my fingers through it, too.

"I loved him, too, *ma moitié*," I start, calling her my other half and knowing she don't know what those words mean. "I lost him, too. You can talk to me."

75

"No!" she shouts, spinning to face me, practically vibrating with rage. "You say you haven't moved on but you have this new job and all these girls ..." Embry closes her eyes tight and then opens them, spearing me with an umber gaze that takes my breath away.

Standing up, I push down the surge of raw emotions in my chest. Naw, I save dat shit for a ring. Not for the girl I like. All these girls, she says. Please. No, there was only ever one girl for me. How can she not know that?

"Do you want me to take the interview questions and type up answers? I could text them to you?"

"No, just ... go." Embry turns away from me and puts her head against the edge of one of her father's bookshelves. "I just want to sleep. I'm tired."

"You're depressed," I say, folding my arms over my chest. I can see her muscles tighten with rage as she whips a glare around at me. I've been facing big mother-fuckers in the ring lately, so it doesn't phase me, but holy shit, dis girl would give them a run for their money.

"Don't talk like you know me, Phoenix. You don't know shit about me anymore."

"Sure I do. Maybe I know you better than you know yourself, you."

"Wow," Embry says, turning fully around and popping out a hip. She plants a fist on it and narrows her eyes, rage burning in dem like the fires o' hell. "Talk

about arrogant. You don't know a fucking thing, Phoenix."

"I know that you broken. I know that you hurtin'. *Ma bonne amie*, whatever shape your heart is, mine's shaped the same way. We both got lopsided organs beating in our chests."

"What are you even *doing* here? Wasn't I clear enough before? I don't *want* to know you anymore, okay? I can't hold onto part of my old life. The edges are too sharp and they cut. Just … let me go and get out, Phoenix."

Embry turns away and sinks into the chair closest to the fireplace, putting her head in her hand.

But still, she doesn't cry.

Moving across the room, I kneel down in front of her and put one hand on her knee.

"Codrick loved you more than anything," I say, my voice fierce. "And he woulda done *anything* to make you feel better, to keep you smiling. But he ain't here anymore, Embry. And you're sick in dat heart o' yours. You need a friend and well, you were da best I ever had, you and Codrick. Let me take care of you, *fillette*."

She raises her head to look at me, a dark shadow falling across her features that I know I can't do anything about unless she lets me. No, she trapped in a cage of her own making. I understand that because I can see my own bars clear as day. Sharp as broken glass. They cut me every damn day.

"Please leave, Phoenix. I don't want to fight." Embry turns her head away from me with a sharp exhaling of breath, her hands still trembling in her lap.

There's not a single part of me that wants to leave her there, but ... I have a fight in a few hours and I won't be able to concentrate if this thing between us escalates. No, better to wait for Monday. I'll be free on Monday.

You know, if I live through dat fight.

"I'm working at my shop tomorrow. It's right on Arbor. You can't miss it, yeah? Come pay me a visit, okay?"

Embry doesn't respond, so I stand up with a sigh, turning to leave before I spin back and put my hands gently on either side of her head.

A single kiss to the scalp, my breath feathering her hair ...

Dat girl doesn't move a *muscle*.

But the trembling in her hands, for just a second dere, it lessens.

"Hope I see you then," I say, and then I turn and leave, praying I don't die on her tonight.

If I did, she wouldn't forgive me in this life or any other.

# EMBRY

## CHAPTER FIVE

I fall asleep in the chair, waking a few hours later to an icy cold that feels like ghostly hands on my shoulders.

Codrick's hands were always warm, so if it is him …

Jerking myself to my feet, I realize the fire's gone out and pad quickly up the steps, letting myself out of the den to the sound of laughter from the living room. The house smells like spices and sausage, beckoning me down the hallway.

My mom is playing boardgames with Jorie and Annamae, my older sisters.

All three of them pause when I come into the room.

"There she is!" Mom says, rising to her feet as my sisters look at me like I'm some sort of science experiment, like why the fuck am I still sad after *sooo* much time has passed. I turn a sharp glare on them that my mom interrupts by stepping between us and putting her hands on my cheeks.

The motion reminds me of Phoenix, of the featherlight kiss he pressed to my scalp and how warm my body got in response to his lips against my skin. We've kissed a few times over the years, but only with Codrick's insistence. When we were drunk, when we were high, on a bet or a dare.

It always felt good, like I was coming home.

That's how I feel now, with that kiss.

And it makes me feel like a fucking traitor.

Love like Codrick and I had only comes along once in a lifetime. Once. That's what makes it so special, right?

"I'll make you up a bowl of gumbo," Mom says, "and some homemade bread with butter. Would you like to come with us to the hospital and take some to Dad? He says the food there is torture. Threatened to leave if I didn't bring a Tupperware container down."

"He also asked for a six-pack," Annamae says, piping up from the floor, a baby monitor clutched in her hand. I met my new niece for the first time yesterday and I didn't feel anything. I'm starting to wonder if I'm even *capable* of feeling anything now. "And we're not bringing him that, are we? Mom, you can't give into his demands. The doctor wants him on a very specific diet."

"Life is short," I say as I move to sit on the couch, looking at my sisters with eyes as hard as steel. I know what I look like. Intimidating. Broken. Unapproachable.

My sisters are both so pretty and frilly, in pink and lavender. Annamae has big dark curls with honey streaks while Jorie has bleached blonde hair that falls to her waist. They've lived charmed lives—even with Annamae's divorce. She got the guy's massive estate in the deal and enough child support that she doesn't even have to *dream* about working for the next eighteen years.

And Jorie? She goes through guys like … well, like Phoenix goes through girls apparently. She never understood what Codrick and I had. When we got engaged at seventeen, she looked at us like we were stupid. Even though our parents got married right out of high school, Jorie was *convinced* Codrick and I would fail.

She didn't even cry at his funeral.

Looking at her now, eyes crinkled with pity, I want to slap her.

"Let Dad eat what he wants."

"Don't start like that, like you've been here the last year looking after him and have a *right* to make statements about Dad's health," Jorie says, and I grit my teeth. She's wearing a pink blouse with a big keyhole cutout over the tits, her lipstick bright pink, her cheeks slathered with way too much blush.

"There's no pre-req required for me to share my opinion," I say, but Jorie stands up with a huffy sigh.

"We've given you a year and a half to get over this," she starts, and my eyes flash with red.

There it is, my most hated phrase in the world.

*Get over this.*

What the *fuck* is there for me to get over?! My fucking soul mate and love of my life is dead. How the fucking fuck am I supposed to just *let that go*? My feelings, my emotions, my love ... it all means something. Who is Jorie to stand there and dictate to me how I should be feeling?

"I'd just stop talking if I were you," I growl out, rising to my feet and clenching my hands into fists. My arms are corded with muscle, and I've been hitting the gym enough to know that I can seriously hurt someone if I need to.

"Are you actually threatening me?" Jorie asks, gasping like she thinks I'd really hit her.

"I'm warning you off before you put your foot so far into your mouth, it comes out your ass."

Jorie's big pink mouth falls open just before Annamae's baby, Lynn, starts to cry, the sound crackling out of the baby monitor in her hand. She rises to her feet, jogging down the hall like there's a crisis or something.

# Baby Girl

Jorie and I stare at each other for a while longer before my mom comes back into the living room and tries to hand me a bowl and a plate with bread on it. I take it and sit back down, my emotions all twisted up inside of me.

*This* is why I didn't want to come back here.

All of this.

The judgement.

The pain.

The … Phoenix.

Phoenix.

Fucking Phoenix.

"Mom," Jorie starts, but my mother shushes her before she digs herself an even deeper hole.

My family doesn't understand.

Nobody does.

Not even fucking Phoenix.

■ ■ ■ ■ ■ ■ ■ ■ ■ ■ ■ ■ ■ ■

There's a three car pileup on the way into the city. Anna-mae finds that out on her phone before we leave for the hospital. Not only is the traffic seriously backed up, but they all know how I react around car accidents.

We take the back way instead.

And when I say *we*, I mean I drive my own car. I can't handle somebody else behind the wheel, not anymore. Back in high school, I would whine and complain if I were made to drive. Now, if someone wants to cart me around, they'll have to pull my cold, dead fingers from this wheel.

Cold dead fingers.

Like Codrick's fingers. Cold and dead. Frozen. One hand on the wheel, the other clutching those fucking roses. Sometimes I wonder if he died because he was holding them in his lap, probably trying his very best not to squash them.

The thought makes me sick.

As we're traveling down a dark, quiet road, dotted with stars instead of suburban lights, I catch a building glowing in the distance. Cars are parked all down the road, lining the muddy expanse all the way to the street.

There's no mistaking the shiny perfection of Phoenix's motorcycle.

My mom and sisters are ahead of me, their lights cutting bright swaths through the darkness.

Making a last minute decision, I put my blinker on —even though nobody's fucking behind me—and pull to the side of the road. As soon as the car is parked and the engine is off, I text both my sisters and let them know I'm stopping at a friend's house to see Phoenix.

They'll probably be confused as fuck, but I don't care.

Opening the door, I let in a frigid blast of cold air, snatch my hoodie and purse from the back seat, and start down the long drive. It winds through trees and around the edge of murky water, dotted with lily pads that catch the waning moonlight.

It's fucking creepy.

"Whoa dere," a man with a shotgun says, stepping into my path and making me swallow hard against a shriek.

He looks like a demon with the silver moonlight limning his hair, his eyes shadowed and dark. But this is the real world, and I know he's just a man. I'm not afraid of men. Maybe I should be, but I'm not. Losing Codrick … that was the worst thing that ever could've happened to me. Death, rape, torture … they seem like pinpricks in the pool of my grief.

Although I *will* protect myself. For whatever reason, I'm still alive. If my life's going to end at any point, it'll be by my own hand.

The man steps closer to me, eyeing my curled hair and tight dress with undisguised interest. I dressed up to go to the hospital again and that seems to be working in my favor right now.

"You one of da girls?" the man asks me, tilting his head to one side. I can see the fat pink slug of his tongue run across his lower lip.

"Yeah." One word, easiest way to keep up with a lie. Like when my friends in New York ask if I've ever had a serious boyfriend. I just say no. It's so much simpler that way ...

"You're late, yeah?" The man takes a step back and sighs, the moonlight cutting across his ragged face. He's scarred to hell with thick stubble and thin lips. He looks at me like a lost opportunity. It makes me wonder. "Hurry up and get in dere," he mumbles, turning his attention elsewhere, forgetting me with one last flick of his shadowed eyes.

Scooting past him, I move into the darkness of the trees once again, the glow of windows in the distance beckoning to me. I can hear shouts and cheers, groans and cursing, all the way from out here. It's so loud and raucous that the sounds nearly drown out the natural calls of the bayou, the chirping of birds and the croaks of frogs, the grunting of gators.

More men with guns appear, staring at me with brutish leers but making zero moves toward me. They don't even catcall to me.

Slinging my hoodie over my arm and hooking my purse up to my shoulder, I head to the open double doors

of the warehouse where two girls in tight dresses and heels taller than mine are standing. Big men with guns stand beside them, faces stoic and eyes scanning the inky blackness all around us. There are *much* nicer cars parked up here in neat orderly rows, and a third woman stands near a locked box with a pair of keys jangling in her hand.

Despite her thick makeup and neon pink dress, I think she's the *valet.*

My eyes take in the Cadillacs and the BMWs, the Ferraris and even a fucking *Bugatti* before I turn toward the girls at the door.

"What?" one of them asks, looking me up and down with a violent sneer. "Are you too stupid to know what *back door* means?" She smirks and flicks a muddy brown gaze over to her friend, a much prettier girl with honey colored eyes. "Or have you ever had a man want to put it in there? You look a little fragile for rough anal."

My lip curls, but I don't say anything.

I have no fucking clue what's going on here, so I just wait. Eventually the two women get tired of snickering and Brown Eyes swings her right arm wide, gesturing along the side of the building.

"Girls go around back. Jesus, you stupid or something?" She rolls her eyes as I move away, staying silent, praying that I haven't made a mistake by coming here. But no, of *course* I've made a mistake. I can't have anything to do with Phoenix Benoit. He stirs up too much of the past and he ... makes me feel weird inside.

But I also know all the trouble his father got himself into—it's what eventually killed him.

If Phoenix is here then he's gotten himself into just as much—if not worse—trouble, and I intend to find out about it.

*Why the hell do you care, Embry?* I ask myself as my heels kick up dirt and dust.

Because ... because I don't know. Because we used to be friends? Because he obviously still cares about me? Shit, I ...

Picking up my pace, I turn the corner and waltz right up to two more armed men, ignoring them completely as I reach for the door handle and let myself inside.

*Jesus Christ, Phoenix,* I think as my stomach crashes to my toes in a block of ice, shattering across the rich rugs laid across cracked cement floors. A chandelier hangs above my head, as gaudy as it is out of place.

"Name?" a woman asks, pausing next to me with an iPad in her arms. When I don't answer right away, she flicks her gaze up and raises her brows. I have no idea what to say, so I play the idiot card, gawping at the chaise lounges and the girls resting on them, dolled up and beautiful—every single one. "Cece?"

"Yeah," I breathe, because I hope this missing Cece girl never shows up here, that she's come to her fucking senses and run for the hills. Beyond the open doorway, I can see a swollen, sweaty crowd, riled up and shouting as two men circle each other in a gigantic fucking *cage*.

*What the fuck is all this?* I wonder as the woman next to me sighs and shakes her head.

"Okay, Cece, follow me." She takes me over to a large safe in the corner, guarded by yet *another* armed man. Taking the ring of keys on her wrist, she unlocks the black door and swings it open, counting out several hundred dollars and passing it over to me. "You get the other half next week."

"Next week?" I croak, because I'm still in shock.

I feel like I've stepped into a fantasy world.

The smell of unwashed bodies and sweat, the copper reek of blood … it invades my nostrils and makes them flare wide as I clutch my hoodie—*Phoenix's* hoodie—to my chest. His smell breaks up some of the stench in the room, that musky spiciness mixed with my mother's mint soap.

"Don't act like the rules weren't *clearly* explained. Half this week and half next week. That's the deal. If you don't like it …" The girl trails off and looks at me with slightly widened eyes, like I better fucking like it because there aren't many alternatives. The man behind her shifts and flicks his eyes over to mine. I hold his stare long enough that he frowns before turning back to the woman with the keys.

"Phoenix?" I ask and she gives a small, private little smile, one that makes my blood boil and turns my hands to clenched fists.

"Everybody likes Phoenix," she says as she gestures with her head, leading me to the opposite side of the room. There's a row of lockers and as I stand there waiting for her to explain, she takes my purse and hoodie and puts them inside, closing the door and locking it with her keys.

Locking away *my* keys.

Trapping me here.

But I have a feeling I was trapped the second I met the first of the hundred fucking armed guys that surround the warehouse.

"Why does everybody like Phoenix?" I ask, trying to pitch my voice to carry over the roar of the crowd. The girl smiles again and I have to resist the urge to reach out and shake her.

"Because he's young. And attractive. And he doesn't take unwilling girls, that's why."

*Unwilling girls.*

Fuck.

"This way," the girl says, clearing her throat and gesturing for me to follow her out the door and into the thick of the crowd. Men and women both jeer and scream, pumping their fists and shouting obscenities as a horrific fight breaks out between the men in the cage. It's brutal, bloody, and awful to watch.

*Phoenix,* I think frantically, searching the crowd for my childhood friend. I can't even *imagine* the boy I grew up with in a sleazy place like this, feeling up girls in too-small bandage dresses and waving cash around as two men beat each other to pulps for entertainment purposes.

It's disgusting is what it is.

No, the Phoenix Benoit I know would *never* bet on something like this.

But … if he had to, he'd fight.

My eyes widen as I spot the big Cajun man leaning against the wall kitty-corner to the one I'm now leaning against, palm splayed wide against the corrugated metal. He's shirtless and sweaty, his tattooed chest rising and falling as he watches the fight in the ring play out, ignoring the shouts and cheers of the crowd. He's tense, and tired, wrapping a white bandage around his right fist, those silver eyes distant and far away.

"Up here, come on!" the girl with the iPad shouts, waving for me to follow her up a set of stairs and along a narrow walkway. There are people up here, too, sitting in balconies that overlook the action but keep them separate from the sweaty masses. Probably the men whose cars were parked out front, the ones driving BMWs and Ferraris and Bugattis.

Their eyes track me as I walk by, like lions searching the savannah for prey.

I feel sick.

The woman with the iPad takes me to a series of seats that protrude over the people in the crowd, spotlights hot and blazing above my head. She parks me there next to a row of other girls who eye me with an even mix of curiosity and hatred. Hmm.

"Wait," I say, grabbing the woman's arm before she can head back down the stairs. "What do I do now?"

She smiles tightly at me and gestures with the iPad toward the cage and the two men fighting inside of it.

"Pray the man you want to win, wins. And that he picks you." She shrugs and moves back down the steps, leaving me there with four other girls and two effeminate looking young men that are as dressed up as the rest of us are.

*Jesus Christ, what is all this shit?*

As I step into the row of well-dressed men and women, the crowd murmurs in excitement, gazes cast in my direction. Money changes hands. My eyes flick to Phoenix.

It takes him a moment, but then he slowly tears his attention away from the ring to look up at me.

Those gray eyes go wide and all the color drains from his tanned face.

Our gazes meet and my breath leaves me in a rush, a connection thrumming between us even in a place as dirty and disgusting as this. A muscle in his jaw ticks as he pushes off the wall and makes his way toward me. Men get out of his way *quick*, and when they don't, he shoves them violently from his path. Heading for the steps, he speaks briefly to the armed guard at the bottom of them, and then scoots past.

"Embry," he breathes as he closes the distance between us, sheer agony lacing his voice. "What da fuck are you doin' here, you?"

"I was driving by and I saw your motorcycle," I shout as he reaches out and grabs my forearms, dragging me close enough that his stubbled cheek brushes my smooth one. Even though he's sweaty as hell, his violet hair plastered to his forehead … he smells good.

"You shouldn't have come here, you," Phoenix grinds out, pressing our faces together. "Lookin' for me? Oh, Baby Girl ..."

The sound of my old nickname makes me stiffen, but this is *not* the time or place to ... fall apart.

"Why are you here?" I growl out as Phoenix pulls away from me, flicking a quick glance to the left, like he's just made a serious mistake by coming over here. "Why are you doing this?"

"I'll win you, me," he declares, taking a step back, his steel colored eyes locking on mine as the armed guard appears behind him, muttering something I can't hear. Phoenix puts a palm to his chest and nods his head. "I'll win you, Baby Girl."

My jaw clenches tight, but when I try to move toward him, the guard steps between us.

"You sit down and wait," he tells me. I bristle at being told what to do, but I'm smart enough not to cause waves when they don't need to be made. Not yet.

Phoenix takes the stairs three at a time and then paces in the tiny walkway behind the crowd, his eyes flicking up to mine every few steps. Raking his fingers through his hair, he turns and watches the end of the fight, tense and agitated, like an animal in a cage.

The bigger of the two men lands on his back with a groan—and he doesn't get up.

*Baby Girl*

The referee lifts up the other man's hand and the crowd goes fucking *ballistic.* Half of them are ecstatic while the other half seem furious.

Phoenix stays rooted to the spot watching as the winner shouts and cheers along with the crowd. He's then given a robe and let out, promptly weaving his way through men and women who shout and congratulate him, clapping him on the back and shoulders.

He comes right fucking for us, up the steps … and then pauses.

"Well, hello there," he says, panting hard and bleeding everywhere. His eyes take me in so slowly that I find myself with my teeth clenched, my hands squeezed into fists. The winner of the fight chuckles and reaches out to touch my chin with two fingers.

Jerking back, I catch Phoenix's wild-eyed stare from below the balcony.

The winner draws his hand back, looking between me and Phoenix, and then mumbles something under his breath, scooping up the blonde in the middle of the row while she giggles and cheers. The man lifts her up like a trophy as the crowd explodes again.

*What* is *this fucking place?* I wonder as the fighter carries off the blonde, pausing to give her a massive, sloppy tongue kiss in front of the entire room. Everyone seems excited about what's happening. Well, everyone but me and Phoenix.

*"I'll win you, me,"* he said.

Win me.

*Win* me?!

Shit, shit, shit.

My eyes flicker back down to Phoenix.

I think he sees understanding fall across my features because he puts the fingers of both hands to his lips and then blows me a kiss. Laughter ripples out all around me, cruel and condescending. I feel like there are weights on my shoulders all of a sudden and I sit back down with a grunt, wondering what the hell I thought I was doing coming in here.

Putting myself up as a … trophy?! A paid trophy?! A whore?!

My thoughts go straight to Codrick, how none of this would be happening if he were still alive. No, if Rick hadn't died on prom night, I'd have spent the evening in his arms instead of on the wet pavement, lying on my side and staring into his glassy dead eyes.

My dress would've ended up in a pool on his bedroom floor instead of lying in a bloodied heap in my bathroom sink for four days before I burned it.

Phoenix and Codrick would've gone with me to NYC. We would've shared an apartment. I'd be happy. I'd be *whole*.

And I wouldn't be standing here wondering how the fuck Phoenix managed to screw up his life so badly. I wouldn't be wondering if *I* was screwing up my life by being here.

There is *no way* these monsters are going to let me walk back out of here.

Sitting there, my heart thundering in my throat, my eyes find Phoenix and stay there. I can't look at anyone or anything else. There is no one and nothing else. And as I stare at him, I can't decide if I hate him for getting me into this mess or … if I … missed him. My heart stutters and slams into my rib cage, making me choke.

The ring is cleaned and prepped for the next fight, the blood and sweat mopped from the floor like it never was. A woman in a teeny bikini walks around the edge of the ring with a sign, just before a man announces Phoenix's name over the loudspeaker.

He makes his way through the crowd and to the front of the room, climbing the steps and entering the cage before casting one last look my direction. He slicks a tattooed hand over his mouth and locks me in place with those silver eyes of his.

*You better not get hurt in there,* I think as I curl my hands into fists and try not to think of the motorcycle crash he got into just *two* fucking months after Codrick died. My mom called to let me know and I swear, if she hadn't prefaced her statement with *Phoenix is okay but* ... I probably would've died right then and there, collapsed to the carpet and curled into a ball of grief. *You stupid idiot.*

Twisting my hands in the fabric of my dress, I watch another man—this big blonde dude with scruffy stubble and wavy shoulder-length hair—take up a position on the other side of the ring. People are screaming, and a voice is shouting over the loudspeaker, but suddenly I find myself unable to hear any of it.

Everything inside of me dims to the even, thundering beat of my pulse. It's going so fast that it fills my skull and echoes between my ears, this sloshing of blood that drowns out everything else around me.

Phoenix doesn't look at me again, exhaling and closing his eyes for a moment. When he opens them back up, there's something missing there in the swirling storm of his gray gaze. He looks empty but sharp, deadly, like a living blade.

Standing there under the hot white lights, I can see every inch of him, all that beautiful ink.

It's hard to see what any those colorful designs really are. There are only two tattoos that stand out to me from all the way back here. The first is the black heart tattoo in the center of his chest, split in half and bleeding red. Big, messy stitches hook the three pieces together, but it's not difficult to see that the whole thing is falling apart.

And the other design?

*RIP Codrick* on his left arm, stretching across the bulging expanse of his bicep. If I were blind, I wouldn't miss that design. It's one of the few pieces with a significant amount of bare skin around it, highlighting the black and gray ink. Why someone would want to carve tragedy into their flesh, I can't possibly understand. Then again, I've driven the design of my own pain so deeply into my heart that I may as well be tattooed, too.

As I'm sitting there gazing with glassy eyes, the fight starts with a sudden burst of energy, startling me.

The two men rush at each other and then circle, throwing out experimental swings of their arms, like they're both waiting for their opponent to make a mistake, leave an opening. Phoenix moves with a predatory grace, this lethal dance of footsteps on the floor of the ring that makes him seem like he's floating. His violet hair is plastered to his forehead, his gray eyes the color of steel, shimmering with the gleam of a freshly polished knife. Just waiting to cut. Just waiting to kill.

I swallow hard because the point of all this isn't for somebody to *die*, right? Nobody is going to die here. It's all about ... a knockout? A pin? Points? I don't have a clue what's going on here. It *looks* like an MMA fight, but ... this is an underground arena with its own sets of rules.

Anything could happen.

Anything.

Breath panting out of me, I look around for a way to escape. Just in case. If Phoenix loses, he'll be okay, right? But he won't get to pick a girl. Isn't that how this works? The winner gets a paid whore all to himself?

But I'm nobody's whore, and if I have to, I'll fight my way out of here.

I'd rather be shot than used.

Closing my eyes, I pray to Codrick. There's nobody and nothing else I'd offer up my private thoughts and hopes and dreams to. God let Codrick die, so screw him. But the love I felt for that man is too impossibly eternal and infinite to have been lost with death. So even if I don't believe in an afterlife or a heaven or a bunch of stupid, often arbitrary rules, I believe in Codrick with *everything* I am.

*Please let Phoenix be okay,* I whisper into the ether. *Watch over him, Rick. He's only nineteen, and you know what it's like to be taken early. You know how many people get dragged down with you. If Phoenix ...*

My prayer comes to an abrupt halt as the blonde man actually manages to land a hit to Phoenix's stomach, making him curl over, his muscles strung taut with tension.

Without even realizing it, I rise to my feet, shaking and sweating, leaning forward and curling my hands around the metal railing.

"Phoenix!" I scream, the sound drowned out by the rumbling of the crowd.

My childhood friend snaps up, eyes flicking my direction. Somehow, I wonder if he heard me. If in this wild chaos, my voice managed to reach his ears. Probably not. Just coincidence. Or ... maybe Codrick.

*Let us get out of here alive,* I pray, imagining Codrick there beside me, his dark eyes shimmering as he reaches up and swipes a few loose tendrils of brunette hair away from my face.

*"I've got you, Baby Girl. I've always got you."*

My body shudders and my eyes widen as the blonde man backs Phoenix into the corner, raining blows down on him. Phoenix shields his face and then abruptly, like a crack of lightning, sends his foot out in a sharp arc, hitting the other man in the gut so hard that he stumbles. He follows up with a hard hit to the man's chin, backing off as his opponent recovers with frightening speed and throws himself into a flurry of wild blows.

Sweat and blood go flying as he hits Phoenix in the side of the face, spattering red across the white floor beneath their feet. My world narrows to a pinprick; the only thing that matters is my childhood friend, the only piece of Codrick Landry that I have left.

Phoenix falls to his knees after a particularly brutal hit to the side of his head and for a split-second there, I think he's going to lose. After all, even promises made in the purest moment of truth can be shattered like glass. Codrick promised me that we'd be together until we were old and gray, that we'd take care of each other, that I'd never have to sleep alone.

All of those promises became lies on prom night.

So Phoenix says he'll win me? That he'll get us out of this mess?

He might not get much of a choice in the matter.

Moving toward the stairs, I start down them, intending to get closer to the fight.

A man with a gun stops me.

"You girls aren't allowed downstairs," he says as he stares at me with blue eyes so pale they look like spider's eggs, white and flimsy and filled with poison.

"I have to pee," I breathe out, feeling sweaty and disconcerted.

My eyes flick back to the ring as Phoenix rises to his feet *and* launches a violent kick, his muscular leg gleaming under the lights, sweat sliding across his tattooed skin. He hits the blonde so hard that the man literally falls back on his ass, succumbing to a fury of Phoenix's fists.

"You can piss *after* the match is over," the man says, blocking my way down the steps with a look on his face that just as soon says he'd put a bullet through my brain as let me go to the bathroom. He doesn't leer at me like some of the other men. In fact, he looks like he'd rather murder me than touch me.

Moving back up the steps, I keep my attention on Phoenix, the light reflecting off his dark violet hair, making it shine purple as he destroys his opponent in a flurry of spattering red. So much blood. So much fucking blood.

If he hadn't recovered, I would've spent more time arguing with the guard, but ...

Phoenix is *annihilating* the other man.

He's hitting him so hard and so fast, I'm afraid he's going to fucking *kill* him.

"First time here?" the brunette next to me asks, leaning close and putting her shoulder against mine in an affectionate sort of bump. "Rules are different than usual."

"He's going to kill him," I whisper, knowing Phoenix too well to think that something like that wouldn't wreck him, tear him apart from the inside out. "Why isn't the ref calling the fight?"

"Not how it works here. It only ends when somebody is unconscious or can't move no more," the girl tells me as I stand there, transfixed by the brutality.

I can't even *see* Phoenix in those gray eyes of his anymore. He's become a fucking animal. Because he's fighting for me? I have no idea, but I have to get to him as soon as possible. Fuck guns and psychopathic stares.

I'm getting over to that ring.

Kicking off my heels, I swing one leg over the metal railing, and then the other. Turning around, I put my arms on the metal bar and then drop down, hanging there for a split second before I fall into the heaving mass of the crowd.

Hands catch me—mostly out of surprise, I think—and then I'm landing unsteadily on my feet, pushing and shoving through the people until I reach the side of the cage.

The blonde man is struggling to get up, managing to get to his feet before he sways unsteadily. Phoenix never lets up, attacking him like a man possessed.

*"I'll win you, Baby Girl,"* he said.

Looks like he intends to do exactly that, no matter the cost.

"Phoenix!" I scream, cupping my hands around my mouth. He doesn't hear me at first, wrapped up in a frenzy of blood and pain. Men with guns stand casually in a circle around the ring while the ref watches placidly from the opposite side. Nobody cares. No, this isn't sport in here. This is brutality. Human suffering as cash changes hands, a transaction in pain and desperation. "PHOENIX!"

My voice tears out of me in a way that's almost painful, wrecking my throat and making me cough.

But it works.

This time, it *works.*

He backs off the blonde man with a sharp flick of gray eyes in my direction, blood draining down the edge of his lip, sweat pouring off his beautiful body in buckets. He's panting, enraged, riled up. He doesn't look like my best friend right now. Instead, he looks like a beast.

His opponent finally finds his feet, takes a wild swing in his Phoenix's direction … and crumples to the ground in a pool of blood.

The ref blows a whistle and the audience writhes and ripples like a storm.

Phoenix stands there staring at me, cutting through the thick heat of the humid air, the metallic taint of blood hanging heavy and pungent all around us. His pulse is hammering so hard, I can see it in his throat, and my own rushes to follow.

*Thank you Codrick,* I think just before the referee grabs Phoenix's wrist and raises it in the air. His eyes, focused on me as they are, are easy to read. I notice his pupils shrinking to slits seconds before a meaty hand clamps around my arm and yanks me back from the ring.

"You fucking bitch," the gunman from the stairs snarls, dragging me backwards.

He doesn't get far.

With a roar, Phoenix is just suddenly there, throwing a punch at the man that literally cracks his front teeth and drops him to the floor with blood oozing from his nose and mouth.

The crowd goes silent as Phoenix steps up close to me and I realize for the first time ever exactly how big he is. He fucking *towers* over me, his gray eyes focused on my face, his breath ragged and wild. The way he looks at me … it's like he's not even my childhood friend anymore.

Sucking in a sharp breath, I find his scent on my tongue—musky, minty, sweet.

Phoenix looks at me the way a man looks at a woman he wants to be his.

Scooping me up in his arms, I find myself pressed to his sweaty chest as the crowd cheers once again and several more guards step up around us. Nobody touches Phoenix though as he weaves his way through the thick heat of the crowd, over to a small door in the back wall.

Yet *another* guard lets us through and then … it's just me and Phoenix in a quiet locker room.

He sets me down on my feet, making me rock with the suddenness of it, and then smashes both palms into the lockers, one on either side of my shoulders.

Phoenix stares at me like he isn't sure *what* to think or say or do.

"We should get out of here," I say, but he looks like a man who's about to come unraveled. Plus, he's literally covered in blood. "Let's get you cleaned up," I choke out, closing my eyes against the sight of him.

My body is reacting in all sorts of strange, inappropriate ways.

There's a violent heat between my thighs, a warmth and a clenching of muscles that I haven't felt in … over four hundred and seventeen days. Four hundred and eighteen days ago, I last had sex. The day before Codrick died. And I haven't felt anything even *close* to this since then.

"Why you close your eyes, *ma moitié*?" he asks me, his voice a husky growl that makes my lids go wide, just so I can see the look on his face while he talks. Sweat draws delicate designs across his blood-spattered skin, but still ... I'm not sure I've ever seen anything so savagely beautiful in all my life. "You know I won't hurt you, me."

"I don't know what *ma moitié* means," I whisper back, trembling so hard, I know that Phoenix can't miss it. But I'm not trembling because I'm afraid.

"It means you my other half," he breathes, leaning close and pressing his forehead to mine.

My eyes close again as my body's wracked with a surge of aggressive emotion.

It flickers inside of me like lightning, lighting up dark places that I never want to look at ever again. I've spent over a year building up my resistance to all of this and ... right now, it feels like Phoenix could shatter it to pieces if he wanted.

"My other half is dead," I say back, quiet and cruel and cold. I hardly recognize myself. Well I fucking should though considering this is the person I've become; this is the way I've survived for four hundred and seventeen goddamn days.

Phoenix's warmth seeps into me, stealing my breath away, melting the sheets of ice around my heart. This

time, when I open my eyes, there are tears, made of melted ice. They leak down my cheeks in cool tracks. Phoenix's gray eyes watch them for several long seconds before he reaches up and scrubs one away with the roughness of his thumb.

He doesn't stop there, trailing his finger along the edge of my jaw, over the curve of my lower lip. I can taste the saltiness of his sweat as our eyes meet again with a jolting shock. My nipples pebble and a whimper escapes my throat, the sound of a traitor.

*I love Codrick; I'll* never *stop loving Codrick.*

But I always loved Phoenix, too.

He's my … my friend.

And he looks like a beast about to go on a rampage.

"Let's get you cleaned up," I repeat when he doesn't respond to my callous comment.

Slowly, carefully, as if I might spook him if I move too fast, I reach up and curl my fingers around Phoenix's wrists, pulling his hands away from the lockers.

"Good fight in there, coon-ass—" a man starts, flinging open the door in the back of the room and then pausing abruptly. He has loose, wavy dark hair and thick messy stubble.

"Get out," Phoenix whispers quietly, turning a slow, predatory look over his muscular shoulder.

The man stares at him for a moment and opens his mouth, righteous indignation scribbled across the handsome banality of his features.

"GET OUT!" he roars, turning around and staring the man down like he could rip his throat out at a moment's notice. If the dark-haired asshole with the ugly scowl didn't have two armed men behind him, I'd believe it.

"Fine. Fuck your whore. But then you and I are going to have a little conversation about Eliette."

*Eliette?* I wonder at the same time the word *whore* rings around inside my skull like the tolling of bells.

Phoenix's lip curls up as I step forward and in front of *him*, like he needs protection from anybody. My eyes are hard as I lock gazes with the dark-haired man and see his curiosity pique. He looks at me like he recognizes me, sending shivers down my spine.

"Hurry it the fuck up," he grinds out, stepping out and slamming the locker room door behind him.

Behind me, I can feel Phoenix breathing heavily, the tension in the air as taut as a bowstring.

Slowly, like I'm turning to face a wild animal, I shift around to look at him, finding his attention already honed in on me, breath panting as blood and sweat drip over his tattoos in streaks.

Without another word, I reach down and take one of his big hands in mine, shivering as memories creep up my back like spiders.

*"When I grow up, I'll marry you both!" I say, smiling as I hold both Codrick's and Phoenix's hands in my own. They're both grinning at me, those big happy stretches of lips that only children know how to do properly. There's no darkness or malice in their gazes, just pure, triumphant joy.*

That's not at all how Phoenix looks now.

His gaze is nothing *but* darkness. Darkness and heat … and want.

He lets me drag him toward the tiled area in the back corner of the room, straight to the showers. Without bothering to move out from beneath the spray, I spin one of the metal knobs and hot water cascades out and over us both, plastering dark hair to the sides of my face, sticking my dress to my skin.

Phoenix makes a sound in his throat, putting his hands on my hips before I can turn around, clamping down with the force of steel in his grip. He leans in close, putting the hardness of his cock against my bottom, making my breath catch as his lips find the hollow between my neck and shoulder, tongue flicking out against my skin and making me groan.

Reaching down, I put my hands around his and gently pry his fingers away. The only reason I can do even that is because he *lets* me. Reaching out, I pump some soap into my palm and turn carefully to look at Phoenix. His eyes are heavy and half-lidded as he stares down at me, some of that rage and anger seemingly draining from him as I rub my hands together and then place a soapy palm on either side of his face.

My fingers and hands trace over every inch of Phoenix's exposed skin, cleaning off the blood as he shudders and tenses under my fingertips, his nipples pebbled and hard ... his cock even *harder.* It's impossible not to notice, standing this close to him.

As soon as the blood is gone and the soap is rinsed off, Phoenix gathers me in his arms and pulls me close, crushing me against his massive muscular chest and making my stomach tighten with knots.

"You shouldn'ta come here," he mumbles, breath teasing my scalp as the water falls over us like a rainstorm, scalding my skin and turning it red. Lifting my head up, I blink through the droplets and find those storm gray eyes simmering with heat. A million times hotter than the shower itself. "You tryin' to save me, you?"

Phoenix leans back and tucks two fingers under my chin, keeping my gaze locked on his.

My body is still singing with need, thrumming with a molten desire that starts between my legs and spirals out to all my limbs, singeing the quiet, emptiness of my heart.

"What have you gotten yourself into?" I ask, my voice husky and breathy and not at all my own. Phoenix slides his hand around to cup the back of my neck and then puts his forehead to mine.

"Tryin' to make things right, dat's all," he growls, pulling suddenly away from me, leaving me gasping and freezing cold, even as the water steams up the air around me.

I step out of the shower and catch a towel that he tosses my way.

"We gotta get you outta here," he growls, low and menacing, drying his violet hair with a quick rustle of his towel. Dropping it on a nearby bench, Phoenix curls his thumbs under the black spandex of his shorts and shoves them down his hips.

Everything inside of me goes quiet and still as I look away and do my best to catch my breath.

Phoenix glances up once and catches my eyes, the long stiff length of his cock standing between us. He growls something in French under his breath and then drags on a pair of *leather* fucking pants, too tight, almost painted on those gorgeous muscular legs of his. He yanks a t-shirt over his head and then tosses me a pair of sweats and a tee that smell just like him.

"Put those on and *quick*."

Turning away, I do as he says, feeling his eyes on me the entire time, heat skimming over the roundness of my ass, the swollen wetness between my thighs, the play of dark hair against my naked upper back. I think I even hear him *growl*, but then my clothes are on and Phoenix is right behind me, shoving my arms into a leather jacket and turning me around so he can zip it up.

"Better than nothin', yeah?" he grumbles, pushing a pair of *huge* tennis shoes on me. His tennis shoes. Dropping them to the floor, I step into them and find it hard to breathe again when Phoenix drops to his knees and ties them tight. "Let's bounce, Embry."

I watch as Phoenix slips into a pair of thick leather motorcycle boots, takes my small hand in one of his huge ones and then drags me back into the locker room and out the door we came through, back into the swollen frenzy of the crowd.

Another fight's just ended, and the winner is up on the balcony between the two effeminate looking men, grabbing a fistful of one's hair and shoving his tongue down his throat.

My pulse is thundering, my body lit up with adrenaline and need as Phoenix takes me around the outside of

the crowd, in the opposite direction from where I came in. Guards are everywhere but nobody pays us any attention except to nod and congratulate Phoenix on his fight.

When we hit the front door and waltz the fuck out of there, I'm in shock.

"Why is nobody stopping us?" I whisper, but Phoenix shushes me with a thick finger to my lips, moving around the corner of the building toward the *back door* that I was herded through.

"What name you give them?" he asks, pushing me gently against the wall with his hands on my upper arms. "Please tell me you didn't give up your real name." His voice is thick with something ... with *pain*. I well recognize that emotion, but I'm surprised to hear it right now, out here in the musty damp of the bayou with nothing but a few shabby orange lights to pierce the darkness.

"Cece," I whisper and Phoenix nods abruptly.

"Don't go nowhere," he growls out, moving quickly past the guards and inside. Standing there with my back to the warehouse, I can *feel* the commotion shaking the corrugated metal walls, making my bones hurt with the amount of violence and greed inside this building. Fortunately, I don't have to stand there long because Phoenix comes back out, my purse and hoodie in his arms. If he notices that the sweatshirt actually belongs to him, he doesn't say anything just yet.

Instead, my childhood friend grabs me by the hand and takes me back the way I came, through the trees, past the murky water and the glint of gator eyes reflecting back silver beams of moonlight.

"Go straight home and I'll follow you there," he barks out as we reach the end of the dirt and gravel drive, pausing next to his motorcycle and my car.

"You'll come in and talk to me?" I ask and although his jaw clenches tight, Phoenix nods briskly. I try to take off the leather jacket and give it back to him, but he stops me with a firm hand on the shoulder, passing me my purse and then slipping into his old hoodie. It's one of the few things I took with me when I left for college in a hurry and I don't know why.

Phoenix waits for me to get into the car and slam the door behind me, watching me through the windshield as I start the engine. He then swings a leg over his bike, kicks it to life, and follows me down the dark road and into the waiting night.

# EMBRY

## CHAPTER SIX

Pulling into the driveway at my parents' house ... makes me feel all twisted inside. Especially when Phoenix's motorcycle grumbles in behind me, igniting memories of nights ... and *people* that are long gone from this world.

My door opens before I even get a chance to turn off the engine, Phoenix leaning over like a shadow. A *hot* shadow whose vibrant warmth curls through the cool Louisiana night and seeps into my skin.

"Lost in thought, no?" he asks me, but *I* am not the one who's going to be answering questions here.

Doing my best to ignore the tension between us, I climb out and duck under his arm, letting him slam my car door closed as I move up the porch steps, my eyes catching on little grooves in the wood where my parents marked my sisters' and my height. Phoenix's and ... Codrick's, too.

Seeing it makes my heart swell, a huge lump forming in my throat. I almost choke on it as I unlock the front door and let us both in. My mom and sisters are still at the hospital—I sent them another text to let them know I was on my way home. Before I even bother to turn on any lights, I send another to let them know I made it safe.

After all, sometimes … sometimes that final text never comes.

I really don't need my dad worrying about whether I got home alive. For some people, that worry is a distant, awful thing, something that they know will never happen to *their* family. Well, it happened to mine and we all paid a price for it.

"Embry," Phoenix starts, closing and locking the front door as I grab a pair of beers from the fridge—Mom will be pissed when she sees them missing, but oh well—and head down the hall. I'm on autopilot, not paying attention to where I'm going or what I'm doing.

So when I open the door to my old bedroom, I feel like I've been punched in the face by a ghost.

Memories assault me, so gloriously golden and full of joy that they poison me, almost cloyingly sweet in the face of my bleak future. The same one Phoenix will share if he doesn't get out of this awful mess he's stum-

bled into. That is, if he even *lives* long enough to have a future.

Spinning around, I shove a beer in his chest, squeeze past him and storm into the den.

Quietly, carefully, he follows me ... but it feels more like I'm being *stalked.*

"Stop it!" I scream, spinning around as Phoenix clicks on the den lights. They're on a dimmer, so they sparkle to life with a low haze that does nothing to banish the shadows from the room. Phoenix's pupils are so dilated right now, it looks like his irises are black.

"Stop *what*?" he growls back at me, twisting the cap off his beer and chucking it on a side table so hard that it bounces right off with a metal clink.

"*Lurking*," I choke out, desperately fighting with the top of my own beer. But my hands are shaking so badly that I can't get seem to get it off, even when I use the bottom of my borrowed t-shirt and wrap it around the neck.

"Give dat over, *ma moitié*," he says, appearing in front of me more quickly than a person should rightfully be able to move. I can see it in the strain of his tattooed flesh over his knuckles, how wound up he still is.

"Stop calling me that," I say as I stare at Phoenix's inked fingers, watching as he twists the cap off with almost zero effort on his part. Our hands brush together as he passes it to me, and then he's just tearing the bottle from my grip and chucking it on the floor.

Amber liquid foams out, soaking the last bit of carpet in the entire house.

"This is the only room with carpet left," I gasp out as Phoenix drops his own bottle and then curves an arm around my waist, yanking me close. "My mom is going to kill you."

"Why?" he growls out, but before I can answer, Phoenix clarifies, his body almost too hot as he presses mine tight against it. "Why you don't like me to call you *ma moitié*?"

"Because … because it makes me uncomfortable, okay?" I say as I drop my hands to Phoenix's chest, palms flat against the hoodie I've been wearing almost daily for … four hundred and seventeen days.

The night Codrick died, Phoenix slipped it over my head.

I've barely taken it off since.

Why?

"I won't say it no more," he grumbles, his chest vibrating under my hands. We're pressed so closely together that I can feel his arousal hard and insistent against me, straining against those ridiculously ostentatious leather pants.

"Let go of me," I start, but he shakes his head. Just once. "What do you mean *no*?"

"I don't wanna let go," he says, closing his eyes for a long moment, the only sound in the room the panting of our wild breaths. "You say it again and I will though." He cracks his lids, gray eyes swirling with an internal storm.

"What the fuck was that place?" I ask instead, knowing I *should* push Phoenix away but finding myself rooted to the spot, the feel and smell of him too familiar to resist. Giving into Phoenix Benoit is like stepping into the past where at least *one* good thing still exists.

"An underground fighting circuit," he says, and that description is so frustratingly vague that I actually *do* manage to give him a shove. It's like pushing against a brick wall. "There are different levels, yeah. What you saw, dat's probably the most minor of dem all …" His big shoulders shrug as my fingers curl into the black fabric of the hoodie. There are tiny holes all over it, and a bleach stain on one arm, but it's one of those things I'd fight tooth and nail to keep. I don't care how many looks I get for wearing it.

There are boxes and boxes of Codrick's clothes in the barn. His mother couldn't bear to have them in the house after he died. I couldn't bear to part with them.

But wearing one of *Rick's* old hoodies? I'd have committed suicide a long time ago.

"What do you mean minor?"

Phoenix growls at me and it's *him* who pushes away
this time, stomping across the now soggy carpet in his
motorcycle boots. For the first time since I handed it to
him, he seems to notice the hoodie he's wearing. Carefully, slowly, muscles strung with tension, he pulls it
over his head and looks at it. There's a second there
where I to pray to Codrick that he won't turn it inside
out, but then he does and I'm just flooded with too many
feelings to stay standing upright.

Sinking down to the edge of the pullout mattress, I
groan and watch as Phoenix rubs his thumb over the tag
near the hood. It still has faded black Sharpie with his
name scrawled across it. The reason was, Codrick had
an identical hoodie, both of them with our high school
mascot—it was a gator, what else?—on the front.
Codrick's mom wrote the boys' names on the tags so
they wouldn't get them mixed up. Not that it mattered,
since they wore each other's clothes on and off anyway.

Phoenix turns slowly to look at me.

"What do you mean by minor?" I repeat, refusing to
acknowledge the emotions in his eyes. They're too var-
ied, a kaleidoscope of pain and ... a dash of hope that I

can't foster. Even if something is happening between our bodies ... I don't have a heart left to give.

If that's even what Phoenix wants.

And what's why I can't look at his face right now. Lust, I can deal with. Erect cocks. Pebbled nipples. But ... it's the emotional stuff that I can't deal with anymore.

"Some nights, men don't just get knocked out. Some nights, they die."

My head snaps up as Phoenix makes his way over to me, crouching low and putting his elbows on his knees. Our gazes lock again, like they're magnetized. I can't look away.

"How did you get dragged into all of this?" I ask, and then it clicks. The new bike. The recessed lighting. The leather couch. "Phoenix, are you doing this for money?!"

"No, no," he says, his voice pained as he leans forward and puts his forehead against my knee. "My Pa got me all mixed up in this. There's money, sure, but I only take it because I can't leave either way." He lifts his head up, laying the hoodie across my lap. "He had big gambling debts, my ol' man. From betting on all d'ose fights, yeah. And when he died ... somebody had to pay 'em off."

"It's not your problem, Phoenix," I choke out, wishing I had the courage to weave my fingers into his dark purple hair and ... and ... offer some sort of comfort. If Codrick were here, he'd know what to do. He'd already have a notebook out, messily scribbling down a plan. He'd stand up and dramatically tack it to a wall, cross his arms over his chest, and raise one dark brow. *"What the fuck are you two waiting for?"* he'd ask.

Me? I don't know what to fucking do.

"This isn't your life," I continue as Phoenix gets up and backs away from me, this feral gleam in his eye, like if he doesn't get out of here, something's going to happen between us whether we want it to or not. And does he? Does he want it? I have no idea. "You don't owe those fucking creeps a damn thing."

I swallow hard and I wonder ... if I'd taken Phoenix with me to New York City instead of pushing him away, would this all have happened? Would I have saved him from going down the same murky path that his father walked? The man lived in the swamp shack he was born in, hunted gators and catfish his whole life, and then died in a bar fight gone wrong. And he left Phoenix with his debts?

It's not right.

Even though I know I *could* and *should* just stay away from all this ... I also know that I probably *won't.*

"I gotta go, me," he says in low tones, his eyes trac-ing over my body with feverish intensity. "Take a shower, go to bed, get up and open da shop in da morn-ing." He closes his eyes, wipes a hand down his face and turns to leave. As he opens the bedroom door, he looks back at me and spears me with a sharp gaze. "Come visit for me lunch, okay?"

And then he's moving down the hall, out the front door. I can hear his motorcycle as it revs to life and speeds off into the darkness.

■ ■ ■ ■ ■ ■ ■ ■ ■ ■ ■ ■ ■

Donaldsonville, Louisiana only ever had one tattoo par-lor in it, and it was a shady shithole with grimy windows and the same faded designs taped to the inside of the glass from the time I was five all the way until … four hundred and eighteen days ago, thereabouts.

Not anymore.

Standing across the street on the sidewalk, I watch as a car with California plates pull up and two young girls with thick shades climb out, blonde hair billowing in the wind. The way they take in the town makes it obvious that they're not from here. Donaldsonville isn't exactly known for being a hopping spot. Basically, there's a historic district and a few church and cemeteries that are somewhat noteworthy.

That's it.

The town boasts a population of about eight thousand people.

But there's only one Phoenix Benoit.

Clutching the handle of the tote bag in tight fingers, I check both ways for traffic—a new habit I picked up in New York. But of course, here in Donaldsonville, there isn't any. Jogging across the street, I hit the new glass door with my palm and it swings inward with the scent of antiseptic and ... something else.

Musk, spice, mint.

Phoenix.

The two girls are standing at the counter, this old-fashioned piece that looks as if it might've been an original piece left over from the buildings stint as a soda shop. Phoenix is standing behind it, smiling as the girls gush about how they drove all the way from Los Angeles to New Orleans and how when they were looking for somewhere to get tattoos, Phoenix's shop—*Wings of Fire and Ash*—popped up online.

"Once we saw your portfolio, we were hooked," the one on the left is saying, pushing her shades up into her hair. She's gazing up at Phoenix like he's the sun and she's a flower who's never seen anything but rain.

And *he* is now looking at me like an *animal* who's spotted his intended mate.

Too many nature metaphors.

"I brought your clothes back," I say, and it's not the *words* I'm saying but the way I'm saying them that scares me. Both girls turn and look at me with expressions teetering between disappointed and jealous. And why? Because I just insinuated that Phoenix and I are either together or had sex recently enough that I have his clothes in my possession.

"'ey Embry," he says, his voice even, controlled, but with an underlying thread of fire that makes my skin feel tight, like I'm trapped inside my own flesh and desperate for a way out. Or desperate to let someone else in? I'm not sure, but I don't like it. "Wait right dere, okay?" He flicks his steely gaze to the two women and smiles, this strange sort of half-smile that's thick with emotion.

I've been here a handful of days and already, I can see that the light-hearted, flirty, playful Phoenix I left behind is gone. Well, I'm sure he disappeared the night we found Codrick Landry lying dead in the rain, but …

My throat clenches and my heart skips an entire beat, making me dizzy.

Using that ironclad control I've spent four hundred and fourteen days perfecting—it's been four hundred and *eighteen* since Codrick died, but for four days, I wasn't even human—I wrap a wall of steel around my emotions, cage them in and drop them in the ice-cold lake of my indifference.

"My receptionist oughta be back from break any minute now. She'll talk over ideas wit' you and when I get back, I paint your skin, no?" He winks at the women which makes them swoon, but really, there's no heat in it. If they can't see that, they're idiots.

Phoenix moves around the counter, stalking toward me in red denim, motorcycle boots, and a black t-shirt that I'm fucking positive belonged to Codrick. It's too small and too tight and now that I'm looking at him wearing it, I'm furious.

I throw the sweats, shirt, and tennis shoes at his chest.

"That's Codrick's shirt," I growl as Phoenix dumps the clothes on the glass coffee table in his reception area and gently curls the fingers of one, big inked hand around my upper arm. "That was in a box in my barn. How did you get it?"

"Let's talk outside," he says as I yank my arm from his grip and storm out, pacing a tight circle on the side-walk in front of the building. "Embry—" he starts, but I cut him off, planting myself in front of Phoenix with the breeze teasing the dark brunette strands of my hair. My reflection plays back at me from the shiny glass win-

dows of his shop, a woman in black sweats and an orange tank with navy blue trim, her face free of makeup, her arms corded with muscle. Her chin is raised in deference but while she tries to look strong, something inside of her is irreparably damaged. Broken. Shattered and unfixable.

The man in front of her looks at her like he's calling her out on her bullshit. He thinks he has glue, that he *can* fix her. But he's wrong.

"Where did you get that shirt?" I ask, pointing at it and trying not to let my hand tremble. I know that t-shirt. I'd recognize it *anywhere.* There's a faded design on the front, the name of Codrick's favorite rock band—*Indecency*—scrawled across it in jagged red letters. All three of us went to that concert in New Orleans, but only Codrick bought a shirt. If I remember correctly—and my memories are a million times more precious than dragon's gold so I horde them—Phoenix bought a hoodie and I bought a tank top.

"Your mom gave all his clothes to me after you left," Phoenix says, raking inked fingers through his purple hair. Standing outside in the sun with him, I can see his tattoos so damn clearly. There's a single red tent tattooed on the upper half of his right arm, a campfire twirling smoke up into a night sky, three figures crouched down around it with their palms out to absorb the heat.

Me, Codrick, Phoenix.

My little red tent that Dad gave us to sleep in.

My eyes narrow and my nostrils flare.

"You took all his clothes?" I ask, and my voice sounds like glass when I speak, jagged and ugly and more than happy to make someone bleed.

Phoenix's face softens as he steps toward me and I move back, closing my eyes against the heat of him, the smell, the size. How did I not notice before how big he was? Or maybe he's bulked up, doing all this fighting. But fuck, he's tall. And his skin is warm and browned from the sun. His eyes are like a stormy sea, and his lower lip is curved and pink and incredibly soft looking —especially since his face is freshly shaved and smooth, making him look *slightly* less animalistic than he did last night.

"Embry, it makes me feel closer to him when I wear his things."

"You can't be any closer to him," I say as I take a step back, trying to control the rage that's welling up inside of me. I don't know why I'm so damn angry. It's not Phoenix's fault that Codrick died. It's not my fault. It's not anyone's *fault*. It was an accident. But how can

something so inconsequential and meaningless as swerving a car in the rain change the fate of so many people?

That night, that rain, that car ... it literally unraveled everything I am inside, left me a tangled mess. I don't know who I am anymore and that upsets me and scares me, and I miss Codrick Landry so bad that it hurts. The hurt makes me mad, but I don't have anyone to direct it at.

Except for Phoenix.

I can throw it all at Phoenix.

"You can't be any closer to him because he's *dead*," I say, swallowing back tears that I refuse to shed. I don't know what came over me last night, when Phoenix got so close to me and my body burned traitorously hot, but it isn't going to happen again. "And when you wear his clothes, you ..."

My hand reaches up of its own accord, fingers brushing down Phoenix's hard chest.

"His smell disappears and ... the colors fade ... and then the clothes get lost or ripped or stained."

My vision is so blurry that I have to blink to make sure I haven't somehow started crying on accident.

"Oh, fuck, Embry," Phoenix says, reaching up and taking my hand in his. He's so goddamn warm, and I hate that I love the feel of his skin on mine so much. It's *comforting* in a way that nothing's been comforting for four hundred whatever-the-fuck days. "You don't need his clothes to remember him, no?" Phoenix tries for a smile, lacing our fingers together. But it doesn't work. Instead, I find myself sick to my stomach but unable to move, my eyes locking on his again. "You just need me. I remember everything."

Phoenix tugs me closer and I stumble a single step forward.

"He smelled like bananas and strawberries because his grandmama made him eat fresh fruit every morning before school. And his eyes were the color of Mississippi mud dredged right from the river. His voice was only half words, but mostly it was laugh. And he loved you more than da earth loves da ocean."

Tearing myself away from Phoenix's grip, I spin and put my back to him, letting the wind catch my long dark hair. It falls halfway down my back, the same brown-could-be-black color that Codrick had. When we laid on our backs together, and our hair mingled, it was impossible to tell whose strands were whose, where one of use ended and the other began.

"Who is Eliette?" I ask, because it's been bothering me all night. It's been bothering me in ways it rightfully shouldn't bother me. Like, why is this Eliette person so important? What does she have to do with Phoenix? Why do I care so goddamn much?

"Eliette dat girl you met," he says, moving up to stand next to me, his eyes almost blue when the sun hits them just right. He doesn't look at me, just stares straight ahead, down a line of historical buildings so pretty they could be plucked right from a postcard.

"The girl you were fucking when I showed up?" I ask, refusing to mince words.

"The girl I was *gonna* fuck, but then, you know, I got interrupted by a wildcat." He turns his attention down to me and *almost* smiles. But there's a heaviness there that's even worse than what I saw last night. Something happened between now and then, and I'm not letting him walk away until I found out what that is.

"Take me to lunch," I say, pointing across the street at one of only two sit-down restaurants in this stretch of shops. My eyes lift to Phoenix's as I exhale, suddenly desperate to move this conversation away from Codrick and back to ... possibly mortal danger, underground crime, and gambling debts. So much easier to deal with than feelings and pain and ... this fucked-up warmth between my thighs that pulses when I get to close to my childhood friend. "And then tell me everything."

I want my head flooded with stories of intrigue and girls named Eliette who make me jealous.

Because if that's what I'm thinking about, I won't be reminding myself that everything Phoenix said about

Codrick was true, that he knew him just as well as I did. The only thing he was missing was the way Codrick tasted, like sunshine and spearmint.

Like the promise of a bright future that could no longer happen.

Not for him, not for me … and maybe not for Phoenix either.

# PHOENIX
## CHAPTER SEVEN

The sunlight streams through the window, catching on Embry's dark hair, da color of chocolate dat is. It takes everything I got in me to stop myself from brushing it back off her face. The way she's glaring at her menu though, I can tell she ain't interested in havin' me touch her.

"Tell me about Eliette," she says, flicking those umber eyes up at me, her mouth pursed slightly. Dat a bit of jealousy right dere? Fuck, I hope so.

"Ain't nothin' to tell," I grumble, closing my menu and leaning back in the booth, crossing my legs at the ankles. "I picked her up once at a club, brought her home. All there is to see what you already saw, you."

"So why does this guy, Roch, think that you had something to do with her disappearance?" Embry asks, pushing her menu to the side and smiling tightly at the waiter when he approaches the table. We place our orders and then sit in silence for a long moment. I trace my finger in the condensation from my Coke.

"Because she gone and disappeared right after she left my house the other night, dat's why." I sigh and rake my fingers through my hair, looking across the surface of the table at the girl I never shoulda let get away.

And after last night?

Holy sweet mother of da lord Jesus, she coulda got herself into trouble. Hell, she almost did. And now, instead of wishing desperately for her to stay, I can't wait for her to get out of here, as far away from this mess I done got myself into.

Hell, I'd go with her if I thought I could but ... that debt of my daddy's, it wasn't going nowhere. And if I tried to run, they'd chase me down. I wouldn't bring that shit down on Embry.

"Shit," she whispers, sucking in a deep breath and tousling her dark hair with her fingers.

"This is bad, Phoenix. Really fucking bad."

"It ain't your problem," I tell her, keeping my voice as low and neutral as possible.

"What's that supposed to mean?" she asks, looking at me with a severe expression. No, dat girl ain't happy wit' me right now. And rightfully she shouldn't be. I've been an idiot, yeah.

"It means I'll tell you whatever you want because I won't lie to you, Embry, but it's not your problem and I don't want you getting involved. You hear me, *'tit fille*?"

"Listen, Phoenix," she says, leaning forward and spearing me with that take-no-shit gaze. Turns me on, but it's not the right time to be thinking about that shit, so I shut those thoughts down. Can't help the thickening of my cock inside my jeans though. "I'm not leaving you wrapped up in all this shit."

"All you doin' is leaving me the way you found me, no shame in that."

Embry's dark gaze narrows on me, but it doesn't take a genius to figure out why she's so angry with me. All my life, I watched my father stumble from one failed venture to another, dig himself so deep into trouble that he never got out of. He took his troubles right to da grave wit' him.

Running my fingers through my hair again, I exhale sharply and try to figure out what to say to make this better. There ain't nothin'. It is what it is.

"I'm sorry I left you before," she whispers suddenly, hands trembling on the surface of the table. As I watch, she curls them into fists and visibly pushes her emotions down. That's not good. Fuck, I want to see her scream and fight, break somet'ing, maybe cry a little bit.

*Like you one to talk, asshole. You haven't mourned Codrick at all, you.*

"You didn't leave me," I growl back, but Embry is closing her eyes and turning her face away from mine.

"I ran like hell," she grinds out through clenched teeth. "As fast and far as I could, I fled and left you behind."

"I'm a grown-ass man." Leaning forward, I curl one of my hands around Embry's arm, drawing her attention back to me. "I coulda made any other choice than what I made."

"Like crashing your motorcycle?" she says, her voice flat and emotionless.

Shit. That night ... I hadn't had da guts to kill myself with a shot to da head or a knife, but ... I'd wanted to die. When dat bike went out from under me, I'd hoped the mercy of the universe was with me. I wasn't thinking clearly, me.

But then I woke up in the hospital and the first thing I thought of was Embry, what I woulda done to her. I'm such a fucking stupid asshole, no doubt about that. If I'da got myself killed dat night, I probably woulda took Embry right along with me to da underworld.

"I'm sorry about that," I breathe, my voice husky and dark. "Dumbest shit I ever did."

She nods briskly and sucks in a deep breath, her hair the color of melted chocolate, dark and shiny and sweet. I want to wrap my fingers up in it, pull her face to mouth, taste the perfect shape of her mouth.

Shit.

I would do *anything* to make her happy. Do I tell her that? I worry that if do, I'm tossing a metal collar around her throat that won't ever let her be happy. Maybe she needs to forget about Codrick, forget about me, and move da hell on?

"So what do we do about Eliette?" she asks, turning her eyes back to mine, their color shimmering with flecks of gold when the sun hits them just right. I can't look away. I trapped, me. So trapped. Trapped in dem eyes.

"We?" I ask as the waiter approaches and sets our plates down on the table. Embry sits still, eyes locked on mine, until he leaves us alone again.

"We," she says, picking up her fork and digging into her pancakes. As she cuts them up, she moves slower and slower, like her mind is caught up in memories. "He made the best pancakes, didn't he?"

"King o' Breakfast," I say and Embry nods sharply, hand trembling again. No doubt she's thinking about Codrick's famous penis pancakes. No joke, dat boy would whip up pancakes in the shape of a long hard dick and balls. He used to cook 'em and make us eat 'em as fast as we could so his mama didn't see. The one time she caught him cooking 'em, she pinched him by the ear and gave him a good talkin' to.

This time, it's my hands that clench into fists, ink straining against my tightened skin.

"If this guy, Roch, if he thinks you've got something to do with Eliette's disappearance, what's going to happen?" I pause and cut into my own pancakes. True to form, Embry and I ordered the same damn thing, down to the scrambled eggs and stuffed hash browns. We always had the same tastes.

"You don't gotta concern yourself with my problems," I say, and she slams her fork down on the surface of the table, some of that old fire in her eyes again.

"Phoenix Avit Benoit, when I ask you a question, you give me an answer, you hear?" I smile and reach out across the table, using my thumb to swipe a small crumb from the corner of her mouth. The way she shivers ... well, it does nothing to stop the painful ache of my cock inside my jeans.

"Yes, miss," I chuckle, and she folds her arms across her chest defiantly.

"So, tell me what will happen if this Eliette person —or another lead on her disappearance—doesn't show up?"

# *Baby Girl*

Drawing my hand back to my lap, I meet her gaze and try on a million ways to say this that'll make it seem less dire. But … there ain't. It is what it is, and if I admit it to myself, I'm terrified. Roch don't like me on a normal day, and if he thinks I had something to do with his baby sister going missing, it's a long walk off a short pier for this asshole.

"In that case," I start, keeping our gazes locked, "I don't have long for this world, *ma moitié.*"

■ ■ ■ ■ ■ ■ ■ ■ ■ ■ ■ ■ ■

"This is a beautiful shop," Embry says, standing just inside the front door and looking around, taking in the red walls, the copper counter … and the framed portrait of Codrick that hangs on the wall to her left. Without hesitation, she moves over to it and pauses, looking at the shelf beneath the frame, covered in half-melted candles and hoodoo charms. I don't believe in nothin'. Why should I? My life ain't blessed. It's hell. What could possibly be waiting for me that's worse than what I already been through?

But … I got crosses and Buddha statues and gris-gris charms, chicken's feet wrapped in twine, rum laced with gunpowder for dat voodoo spirit, Baron Samedi.

It's all silly nonsense, sure, but ... it makes me feel better.

"You have a shrine," Embry says, but her mouth quirks into a sad smile. "Codrick would've loved this; he was a cocky bastard."

A woman's heels preceded my receptionist, Priya, as she stepped out from the curtain behind the register. Tall, lanky, with a short dark bob, brown skin covered in ink, and pale chestnut eyes, she stood out in this part of Louisiana. Couldn't go a day without seein' her get hit on by some creep or another. I've had to kick alotta ass over dis girl and we never even fucked.

"Who is this?" Priya asks, leaning against the wall and giving Embry a very careful once-over. "Instead of taking a girl *out* of the shop, you brought one in? That's a shocker."

"This Embry," I grumbled out, reaching up to scratch at the back of my head.

Priya's been around since I opened the doors three months ago; she knows all about fuckin' Embry.

"Oh," she says, her eyes sparkling as she stands up and makes her way over to the much shorter woman. "*You're* Embry."

"I take it you've heard of me and Codrick?" Embry asks, leaning forward and putting her cheek playfully against the painting. Seeing her cheek to cheek with the dark-haired asshole in the picture, it makes me sad. So fucking sad.

"Every little detail," Priya says with a smile, pulling a lighter out of her leather pants and flicking the wheel. "I light candles and incense for him every damn day." She hands Embry her lighter and watches as my childhood friend lights them all up with a sharp intake of breath. "What brings you to town?"

"My dad's in the hospital," Embry says, putting the lighter aside and dipping her head like she's prayin' somet'ing fierce.

*"She's talking to me, you know,"* Codrick says, standing on my right, leaning against the old soda shop counter with a grin. *"When I was alive, I could make her sing hymns, call out Oh God! in bed, and now ... now she prays to me. What do you think about that?"*

"I think it's real-real sad," I whisper aloud, but fortunately nobody hears me.

"That's right—Phoenix mentioned that. Devin is your dad, right?"

"Yep," Embry says, lifting her head up to glance back at me. "He had a minor heart attack." She moves over to the counter, running her hand along the surface of it and walking right through the imaginary ghost of Codrick Landry. She pauses at the small stack of books in the corner and starts flipping through them, looking at pictures of my art.

"Well, Phoenix talks about you all the damn time. I'm sure he's *thrilled* to have the love of his life in town."

"The what?" Embry asks, stiffening and spinning to face Priya.

"His … oh shit," she mumbles as I narrow my eyes and clench my jaw tight. "I thought that was common knowledge …"

"He …" Embry starts, choking on emotion. I know well dat face.

I move toward her, but she backs up and scoots around me.

"I'm staying here until you get off work," she says, taking a seat on the sofa near the window and pulling out her phone. "Just do your thing and … then we'll do ours."

"Whoa," Priya breathes, but I know there's no way in hell that what she thinks is happening is gonna happen.

Embry got eyes for one man only … and he's as dead as I'm gonna be if I don't figure my shit out.

Whether she likes me the way I like her, *love* her, or not, that doesn't mean shit.

# Baby Girl

I can't and won't let Embry LeBlanc feel pain ever again, so long as there's a heart beating inside my chest.

# EMBRY

## CHAPTER EIGHT

Watching Phoenix work is … mesmerizing. His smile is magnanimous, and the way his eyes shine as he inks his beautiful art into his customer's skin … It makes my heart hurt in ways that I refuse to acknowledge.

Because I've felt those pains before and … we each only get one chance at love, right? Just one perfect chance, and I lost mine.

Closing my eyes tight, I block out the sight of Phoenix with black gloves stretched over his hands, a beautiful girl laid out in his chair. *Good God, Codrick, I can't let anything happen to him. The three of us were everything to each other, and … we were all Phoenix ever had. We were his family. I need your help.*

Flicking my gaze open, I continued to play around with my phone, going through pictures of people back at school, people who meant nothing to me in the scheme of things. Being here with Phoenix was a good reminder of that, of what a *true* friend felt like.

# Baby Girl

To be fair, I'd never given any of the girls back home a chance, not really. My heart is closed for business, locked down tight in shackles of my grief's making. I'm a prisoner of my own emotions, that much is obvious. Somehow, seeing Phoenix makes all my short-comings seem so glaring, like how could I have missed them for so damn long?

Curling up on my side, I put my head on a pillow and tuck my phone against my chest. I have *one* picture on there with Codrick and Phoenix, just one. And it's from that morning, that morning before he crashed his car and lost not one ... but *three* lives in the wreckage.

Tears prick underneath my eyelids as I shut them tight, but I refuse to let a single drop fall. Instead, I let the merciful arms of sleep take me ... and wake to a gun pressed against the side of my head.

▬ ▬ ▬ ▬ ▬ ▬ ▬ ▬ ▬ ▬ ▬ ▬

"Get the fuck up," a voice orders gruffly, and I come to, waking from ... a nightmare to another nightmare. Without looking over to see who's talking to me, I sit up and slip my phone into my hoodie pocket at the same time I rise to my feet.

Standing up in a situation like this never makes things worse. I'd so much rather be up and awake than lying curled on my side asleep. This asshole's the idiot for forcing me to alertness.

Phoenix is standing across the shop, bloody and leaning against the wall next to Codrick's picture, candles flickering and casting an orange and yellow glow across his face. His jaw is clenched, and his fists are balled so tight it looks like the tattoos there might peel off and go dancing across the shop floor.

"You left last night when I fucking told you I wanted to talk. And then you think you can fucking hide from here?"

"Who said I was tryin' to hide?" Phoenix spit out, swiping his hand across his bloodied jaw and clenching his teeth tight. "I'm at work, you fuckin' mud for brains dumb shit. Ain't nobody trying to hide."

"No?" the dark-haired man in the shitty suit, Roch, pulls back the hammer on his gun and my heart leaps into my throat. "We found my sister's body not a hundred feet from your fucking swamp shack. You want to explain that to me?"

"That ain't possible," Phoenix says, standing up and leaning his back against the wall, like he's hurt when I can see in every muscle of his body that he's okay, tightly leashed violence ready to explode. "If she were laying out dere for dat long, the gators woulda got her."

Roch swings his gun out and hits Phoenix across the face, spattering blood across the wall. The big Cajun man just stands there and takes the beating. He doesn't look at me which is probably a good choice. These guys are definitely not above using me to get at him. I can already feel my heart thundering, my mind spinning for schemes on how the hell to get out of this.

I don't sense this confrontation winding down to any sort of amicable conclusion.

Flicking my eyes to the right, I only see two guys— the one with the gun on me and another with his gaze fixated on Phoenix. They expect him to roll over and play dead looks like.

"Whatever the case, you're going in the cage tonight. If you survive, then you can argue your point," the man says, stepping back and smirking. I hate him with a violent intensity in that moment, an almost impossible rage that sneaks up and bites me in the ass. My hands curl into fists and I stare at this man, taking advantage of Phoenix's easy-going nature. What other man would give two fucks about debts that his father owes?

Not many.

"Send me to the cage. I don't care none."

"Of course you don't," the man sneers, but he way he looks at Phoenix doesn't seem right for the scenario. He hates him, sure. He wants him dead, maybe. But he isn't looking at the much bigger, much more muscular man like a murderer. No, he's looking at him like he's ... jealous? Uncomfortable? I have no idea. But he's less interested in finding out who actually killed his sister than he is on pinning her death on Phoenix. "But I think you'll care if we drag your new whore back there and bend her over one of the sponsor's knees, huh?"

"Put me in the cage instead," I say, lifting my chin up and crossing my arms over my chest. "I saw women who *weren't* wearing teeny-bikinis last night, girls who fight. Let me go all in, and I'll beat the odds."

"You?" the dark-haired man asks as Phoenix clenches his teeth and gives me a look that clearly says *shut the fuck up*. "You'll get that tiny ass ripped in half and handed right back to you. Nah, you'd be better off on your knees."

"I can fight," I said calmly, relaxing my hands at my sides. I don't know why I'm doing this. "And I'll win you a shit ton of money. Everyone will bet against me."

"You're so full of shit—"

"If I win, you report your sister's death to the proper authorities and let them handle it." Exhaling, I lift my chin up and stare this guy in the face. There is no way in *fuck* he's going to do what I'm suggesting, but I have a feeling that if I don't get Phoenix out of this mess, something worse is going to happen. I need to buy us some

time. "Phoenix and I will win tonight," I repeat. "You like money, right? Let us earn you some. And then you can find out who *really* hurt your sister."

I'm panting now, because I know guys like this. I've seen them many times before. Here, in New York. They think they own the world.

"Fuck you," he says, seconds before I send my right elbow out and into the throat of the man holding the gun to my head. His weapon flies up and fires into the ceiling before I sweep a kick and knock him on his ass. He drops the handgun at right about the same moment the other man points his at me and puts his finger on the trigger.

"See what I can do?" I whisper as the guard's hand tenses and I hold my palms up and out. *I could very well die right now,* my mind breathes, and instead of feeling … numb towards it, I feel sick to my stomach.

I need to protect Phoenix.

That's the only thing that matters to me in that moment.

"She don't gotta do this," Phoenix says, standing there next to Codrick and looking fierce as fuck. I don't doubt that he would kill all three of these men to get me out of here. But … even worse things would happen to him—both inside and out. I won't let him kill a man nor will I risk him getting in even deeper into this mess.

151

"I want to," I say, reaching up and slicking my hair back. "And I can."

The dark-haired man relaxes slightly and I know I've got him right where I want him. He wants Phoenix gone, for whatever reason, but he also likes money, and he's confident he can take care of him later.

There won't be a later; I'll make sure of that.

"Embry," Phoenix says, his voice both a warning … and a promise.

The look I give him in return is both of those things in equal measure.

We're getting out of this together.

<hr />

The noise of the warehouse is overwhelming, sweeping over me in waves as I lean against the wall and cast my eyes over to Phoenix. There are numerous armed guards between us, and I know without even having to be warned that we won't be allowed to talk.

In his gray eyes though, I can sense his frustration and pain and regret.

He never should've let me stay at the tattoo shop with him.

He never should've let this happen.

Glancing away, I exhale sharply, running a palm down my bare belly. I'm dressed in a tube top and short-shorts, wraps around my ankles and wrists. I've never done anything like this before, but I have been taking self-defense classes in New York. A person can only run on a stationery treadmill for so long before they go insane. I'm strong, and I've picked up some tricks, and … I just know that I better not lose here tonight.

*Watch over and protect us tonight, Codrick,* I pray as I flick my eyes back to the ring. The woman on the ground right now is *twitching.* That can't be good. Swallowing past a sudden lump of fear, I stare at the winner, rippling with muscle and screaming at the top of her lungs.

Fuck.

The same routine as last night—the ring is cleared out, all that blood washed away, and then the girls in the bikinis with signs start walking around the announcer calls out a brand-new fighter for the night.

The crowd boos, but I don't let that bother me. Mob mentality is a sick and terrifying thing. But they'll see, and they'll be sorry they bet against me.

The guard nearest me stands up straighter, and I take that as my cue to start forehead, weaving through the sweaty, hot mass of spectators. As I weave my way through them, this deep sense of rage fills me, just like it did in Phoenix's tattoo parlor. If they didn't thirst for this blood and this pain, we wouldn't be here right now.

Their need for violence and pain is what's fueling this machine.

As I ascend the steps into the ring, I wonder if I should've called the cops last night. But hell, out here, whoever runs this thing has probably got the damn cops in the palms of their hands. No. I don't need to stop these people from doing what they want to do. My only goal here is to free Phoenix, and then ...

I can go back home to New York and pretend like none of this happened?

Doubtful.

Phoenix is making me feel ... unraveled, all those strings I'd wound up and tucked into dark places, they're being ripped out and tied into awful knots.

Standing in the ring is a transcendent experience. I can feel the eyes of the crowd burning into him, digging deeper than they ought to be able to. They're trying to crawl inside of me and see what makes me tick, find my cogs and gears so they can claw them out and watch me fall apart.

Across from me, there's a young woman with her short blonde hair pulled back and braided into tight narrow rows. Probably so I can't pull it. My own hair ... might be a liability. But Codrick *loved* my hair. He ...

would lay next me for hours while we talked and run his fingers through it.

That and … I can't get over Phoenix grabbing a fistful of it in his fingers and breathing it in, taking in my scent and lifting heavy-lidded eyes up to look at me.

Mm.

Phoenix, fuck.

Exhaling sharply, I block out the noise of jeers and catcalls, bets and drunken scream. I breathe through the hot sticky smell of sweat and unwashed bodies, the dual scents of copper from all the bloodshed and bleach from cleaning it up.

My opponent stares me down and narrows her eyes, that pale blue gaze taking me in like I'm less than nothing, an insect to crush beneath her heel. And that's how I have to see her, too, if I want to get through this.

The ref calls the fight and I just stand there for a moment, my mind flickering back to Phoenix and how he started his own match. I remember the men circling each other, so I do the same, following the other woman's other steps.

We're not even halfway around the circle before she lunges for me, hitting me so hard in the stomach that for a second there … I'm sure it's already over. I can't breathe and the pain … oh *God*, the pain!

But I've survived worse.

So much worse.

Seeing Codrick dead was the worst thing that ever happened to me. Losing Phoenix would be the second. Or ... maybe it would tie. I don't know. I don't know.

And I just need to get us out of here, so I can find out.

Swinging blindly, I manage to clock the other woman on the chin, knocking her back a few steps. She doesn't let that faze her though. No, within seconds, she's coming at me again, dropping low for a kick that knocks to my knees. Her knee isn't far behind, coming for my chin.

The hit she gets to my face ... it scrambles my brains, and I swear, I can hear Phoenix roaring somewhere in the crowd. I let that sound infuse my blood, throwing myself against my opponent's legs and knocking her to the ground with me.

We wrestle around and although I can tell that she's well-trained in what she's doing, practiced, confident ... I'm stronger. I'm strong as hell. Every day, all day for four-hundred and eighteen days, I've worked out. It's basically all that I do besides study. I don't watch TV or read books or hang out with friends—I tone my physical form. Why not, since my spiritual and mental forms are complete disasters?

# Baby Girl

The blonde girl grabs hold of my hair and pulls with so much force that tears spring to my eyes. The crowd goes ballistic at the image of her sitting on my back, straddling me as she yanks on my hair so hard, I feel like either my skin is going to peel off my skull or else my back might break.

With a scream of rage, I twist my body to the left and even though it hurts like fucking *hell*, I manage to dislodge the bitch from every part of me except my hair. Ignoring the sensations in my scalp, I fling myself on top of her, letting her fingers get tangled in my hair. I throw out punches the way Phoenix did to that other guy, swing after swing that connects with a sickening crunch, blood spurting everywhere.

Even as I'm doing it, I'm horrified by the scene.

That thought makes me hesitate. It's only for a second, but my opponent is a professional, throwing me off and letting go of my hair. While I'm still struggling to my knees, she's already on her feet, sprinting over and kicking me as hard as she can in the side. It feels like I've been hit by a truck.

My stomach contracts with these awful, forced coughs, and I feel like I might puke. Everything is spinning, and adrenaline is rushing through me, making me dizzy and unstable. That's when I realize what an idiot I am. I might actually lose this fight! And then what? Then what?!

Fuck, fuck, fuck, I didn't think far enough head! My plan isn't going to work. Phoenix is going to die. Just like Codrick, the universe is going to snuff him out of existence.

*"Baby Girl," Codrick says, lying there on his side and looking at me with dark, soulful eyes. "Get up. You've got this." His smile softens and he reaches out to brush some hair off my forehead. "Fight for Phoenix. We love him too much to let him go."*

Looking at a ghost, one who's clearly stirred up from the pain fragmented nightmare of my imagination, should rightfully have me on the ground sobbing. Instead, I throw myself to the side and barely manage to avoid another blow. Scrambling upright, I put all my body weight into the move and rush my opponent.

If this were a real MMA fight, I'm sure I'd be disqualified like a million times over, but that's not what this is. This is a vision scramble to the death. Well, not literally—not tonight anyway—but close enough.

The woman stumbles back, reeking of sweat, her skin slippery with droplets of sweat and blood as I wrap my arms around her and knock us both to the ground. My victory doesn't last long as she quite literally *kicks* me off and sends me rolling across the ring again.

# Baby Girl

This time, I get to my feet quickly enough to fend off another barrage of attacks, bouncing around to avoid a rapid flurry of arms and legs. She thinks I'm tired and hurt, that I'm not much of a threat, and she's trying to finish this thing *quick.*

That's her mistake.

Time works strangely in the ring, with all those hot-white lights, a hostile crowd … Phoenix's silver eyes. I have a feeling that if I found myself on the ground, being pummeled to a pulp, that he'd rush through the crowd and rescue me. Might get himself shot in the process, but he'd do it.

As soon as there's a break in my opponent's flurry of moves, I rush in and strike, using an uppercut on her chin that knocks her head back and sends her stumbling. I'm not a violent person at heart, but neither is Phoenix and he can kick anyone's ass. We do what we have to do, I guess.

Swinging my leg up, I mimic the move she threw at me earlier and hit her in the stomach with all the strength I have. The woman gasps and stumbles back onto her ass, but I go down, too, thrown off-balance by the kick. Picking myself back up, I spin just in time to block her, watch her bounce back for another flurry of attacks, and then throw every last ounce of power I have left into another punch.

My fist hits her face and she crumples, falling to the ground in a groaning pile.

She doesn't get back up.

As I stand there panting and shaking, I wait for the ref to call the fight.

*I ... won,* I think as I quiver and shake, letting him lift my bruised and blooded hand in the air. But the crowd isn't happy that I've won. No, everyone was betting against me.

It takes two guards to get me to the edge of the crowd where both Roch and Phoenix are waiting.

My friend's gray eyes lock on mine and something passes between us, hot and vibrant and unstoppable. But I can only hold his gaze for a moment it's so intense, switching my attention over to Roch, smirking and scratching at the stubbled hair on his chin.

"Fuck, guess you did make me some money." He tilts his head at the winner's podium. "Pick a prize and get the hell out of here." I glance up and find a row of men and women, just like last night.

"I'll take him," I say, pointing at Phoenix and the dark-haired throws his head back in raucous laughter.

"Whatever. If he wins his fight, sure, you can fuck him." Roch pauses and looks hard at me. "Get her out of here, she stinks."

The guard tears a door open and shoves me into a locker room.

No, not *a* locker room, but the same one from last night.

Running my fingers through my hair, I pace the floor, shaking and shivering, the adrenaline draining out of me and the pain rushing in like a tsunami. Everything on me hurts—my legs, my tummy, my arms, my head.

Groaning, I sink down on the bench and try to take a few deep breaths.

My plan was spur of the moment and now ... I don't know what to do with myself. The thought of *not* watching Phoenix fight makes me anxious and I start to pace, even as I'm groaning in pain. Tomorrow, I'm not going to be able to *stand*.

Creeping over to the door, I tug the handle and find it ... locked.

Figures.

Immediately, I try the other door, but it's also locked. A quick round of both the changing area and the showers reveals absolutely no other exits, and the only window I can see is about thirty feet up. The chances of being able to get up there ... slim to none.

Sitting back down on the bench, I close my eyes and listen to the crowd. Phoenix seemed to be a favorite, so when I hear them cheering, I imagine that they're cheering for him.

"Please, please, please be okay," I whisper, steepling my hands together and putting them against my forehead. My entire body is quivering, my heart thundering, and all I can think about is Phoenix's warm body pressed against mine in the showers, the hardness of his cock grinding against my ass.

*The love of his life in town,*" Priya had said.

Meaning me.

I'm the love of Phoenix's life?

The thought makes me … uncomfortable to say the least. Digging my fingers into my hair, I prop my elbows on my knees and I wait. And wait. And wait.

Just when I'm sure I'll have no other choice than to scale the thirty feet of corrugated metal wall behind me, the locker room door opens … and there he is, covered in blood and quivering twice as badly as I am.

"Phoenix," I whisper as he storms across the room and grabs me by the back of the head with one of his massive hands. His lips slant over mine and the entire world just … stops.

There's nothing in my universe but his warm, bloody fingers on the back of my scalp, his lips massaging mine, his sweaty, shirtless body pressing close. Phoenix parts my lips with his tongue, taking over my

mouth with long, hot sweeps, making my knees feel weak. I'm so relieved to see him, so drained from the fight, I swear, I almost collapse to the ground right there in front of him.

Instead, he bands an arm of steel around my waist and pulls me close, kissing me with so much passion and heartache and rage that I feel tears peek at the edges of my eyes. I haven't been kissed like this since … Codrick. His kiss was everything: the air I needed to breathe, the heat I needed to stay warm, the passion I craved.

Phoenix's is … it's …

Turning my face away from him, I cut our kiss short.

Even though it's brilliant.

Even though it's *everything*.

"We need to figure out how to get out of here," I whisper, even as I feel his hardness press against my belly, feel my own traitorous insides tighten and flutter, desperate to feel him inside of me.

"You stupid sometimes, Baby Girl," he chokes out, and even though the sound of Codrick's nickname of Phoenix's lips makes me sick, I close my eyes and lean against him. I'd rather have my boundaries tested than lose the only friend I have left, one of only two best friends I've *ever* had. "We'll talk about how stupid dis plan was later, yeah?"

"It wasn't stupid," I murmur back, looking up into eyes the color of a storm. Hell, they have the same intensity as the storm, too. I want to get lost in them; I want to drown. Shaking my head, I clear that thought and try to take a step back.

Phoenix refuses to let me move, keeping me in place with the strong, hard pressure of his arm around my waist.

"I got an idea," he says, pressing a kiss on my forehead that ... does all sorts of weird things to my insides. Phoenix rubs his stubbled chin against my head, giving me the chills, making my nipples hurt they peak so fiercely. "And a much better one than you lettin' yourself climb into dat ring."

"I kicked her ass," I whisper, and he laughs, the sound traveling through me as Phoenix steps back and starts opening locker after locker until he finds what he's looking for.

"You got lucky, you. Just da right girl, da right circumstances, and da right amount of spunk." He snatches a hot pink dress and some heels from the locker, tossing them over to me just before jogging into the shower area and returning with a damp towel while I stand there dumbfounded. "Let's get you cleaned up and into dose clothes. Quick, *ma moitié.*"

I'm too nervous, too full of jitters to argue. Besides that, my lips hurt. They feel like they've been stung by a thousand bees, tingles flittering through me that I don't know what to do with. Because liking Phoenix the way I liked Codrick … feels like a betrayal. It's a betrayal of the worst kind, isn't it? Sullying his memory like that?

*"You know I want you to be happy—whatever that means."*

The words of my deceased fiancé ripple through me as Phoenix carefully, almost sensually cleans most of the blood off. And because there's no time and because this just isn't the place to care about nakedness, I strip down, kicking off my shoes, shoving my shorts down, tearing off my top.

Phoenix steps forward, lifting the pink dress up. With a sharp intake of breath, I lift my arms in the air, making my nipples feel extremely exposed, gasping when Phoenix gets too close and they brush against his bare chest. It's tanned from the sun, scarred from his bike accident, and covered in ink.

I want to touch it so goddamn bad.

He pulls the dress down slowly, letting his big, rough hands brush against my breasts and hips as he goes, yanking the fabric into place as his fingertips dance across my upper thighs.

"Shoes," he growls, bloody and fucked-up, with his violet hair plastered to his forehead with sweat. "Let's go, *'tit fille*," he whispers, dropping to one knee and using big, shaking hands to slip my feet into the pink heels, like I'm some fucked-up version of Cinderella or something.

When he rises to his feet, I feel like he's just towering over me, this massive structure of muscles and rage and … an infinite amount of gentleness when he reaches out and brushes some hair from my face. He cups my cheek in one big palm and brushes his thumb over my tingling lips.

"You gonna have some bruises in da morning," he whispers, kissing me hard on the mouth. It's not the same kiss as last time. This one is possessive and male and completely unlike anything I've ever felt before. Codrick wasn't … he wasn't as *wild* as Phoenix.

"It was worth it," I say, lifting my chin in defiance as Phoenix drags on a black t-shirt and then grins at me. An undignified squeak escapes as he scoops me up in his arms like I weigh nothing and carries me over to the back door, the one Roch had come in the night before.

And then he waits.

"What are we doing?" I ask as the door swings inward and Phoenix pushes forward without answering me, shouldering past a big man in a t-shirt and jeans.

"Didn't know you were fighting tonight?" he says as Phoenix tosses him a big Cajun grin and winks.

"You know me, I get a taste o' somethin' I like and dat's dat." The other man grins back at him and then the door is swinging closed and we're alone in an empty hallway. Phoenix doesn't bother to put me down, moving quickly down the narrow space and into another room, this one occupied by a few men sitting around a table and drinking, girls on their laps, cigarettes in their mouths.

They all have guns by their sides, but nobody's touching them.

"Crowd is awful fierce," Phoenix grumbles as a few of the men glance at him, studying my body appreciatively. "Me, I just wanna have a moment wit' my girl outside." He smirks, and for a second there, I can almost believe that in another life, he'd be the pathetic misogynistic asshole he's pretending to be. But ... no, no, this is Phoenix Benoit, gentle giant. I mean, he *is* kind of an asshole, but there's this humane core inside of him, this inner goodness that most people don't have.

Dropping me onto my heels, Phoenix curls his right arm around my waist and drags me roughly to a back door, kicking it open and slipping outside into the cool bayou night without so much as setting off the alarm.

But I remember last night.

We did the very same thing and they came hunting for us. This time ... I have a feeling it's going to be sooner than we'd like before somebody realizes we've escaped. We head off in the opposite direction to the road that we came in on, stuffed in the back of an SUV, staring at each other but unable to talk.

It gave me strength, though, being able to look at him like that. He really is a beautiful man with jaw bones that taper into a strong chin, a wide but straight nose, full lips surrounded by blonde stubble.

"We got minutes at most ... maybe seconds." Phoenix takes me all the way to the edge of the swamp and then turns to me. "Kick off your shoes, take off your dress. It's too bright." He tears his t-shirt over his head as I gape at him, but do as he's asking. I figure he's probably right. And if we get caught ... I don't want to imagine getting caught.

Shedding my shoes and dress, I yank the tee over my head as Phoenix wads the clothes up and tossing them into the murky swamp water. Taking my hand, he leads me into it and I shiver at the cold. Everyone thinks Louisiana is warm, and it is ... in the summer. It's fucking winter right now and the nights are cold.

We wade in ankle deep, knee deep, waist deep.

I shiver at the cool water and the murky filth under my feet. There are snakes out here, and gators, spiders,

mosquitoes. It's sort of one of the last places I'd want to be in the dark.

One of.

I'd much rather be here than inside that warehouse.

Once he starts swimming, Phoenix lets go of my hand.

"Grab onto my neck," he grumbles, but I refuse, swimming alongside him and listening to him curse in French. "You're the most stubborn girl, *ma moitié.*"

"Like you're much better?" I whisper, our voices swallowed up in blackness, the night sounds of nature providing a soft, comforting filter. Okay, so yes, we could theoretically *die* out here from a poisonous snake bite or something, but our chances were infinitely better here than inside the walls of that warehouse. Besides, a snake wouldn't rape me before it killed me which could very well happen with Roch and his men. "Where are we going?" I ask as we continue swimming, pausing to rest on the mossy edge of a small island.

At this point, I'm fairly certain Roch's men won't be able to find us. Fuck, I'm sitting right here and *I* couldn't find us if I tried.

"Paw-Paw's hunting cabin," Phoenix says tiredly, scooting closer to me and putting an arm around my waist. Even though we're both shivering, as soon as I touch him, a surge of warmth spirals through me.

"Nobody go'n' find dat place without my help." Phoenix drags a hand down his face and then pauses to shimmy out of his *pants*.

"What are you doing?" I choke out, the sight of his cock in the moonlight far too appealing to admit. We're freezing to death in the middle of the bayou, running for our lives, and I'm looking at my best friend's junk?

*Codrick, help me*, I groan as I look away and Phoenix chuckles.

"It's wet and heavy and it isn't doin' shit to help me stay warm. We're not gonna run into anyone on our way to da cabin, and I got extra clothes there." He reaches out and tugs at the soggy sleeve of my tee. "If you want to take dis off, I promise not to ravage you until we get to the cabin."

My cheeks flush, but I roll my eyes, as if he's joking with me.

I'm pretty sure he's not.

"I can't ..." I start, but then *something* slithers past my feet and I choke back a scream, tucking my knees up against my chest as mosquitoes buzz around my ears. There's just enough moonlight for me to see the smirk on Phoenix's face.

"You got a swamp rat to lead you to safety, Embry," he says, sliding back into the water and then turning

around to tap at his shoulder as he treads water. "Climb on and I'll give you a ride, me."

"I can swim just fine," I say as I slid in beside him and he gives me a look. "Surprised? I took classes in New York."

"You live in Louisiana your whole life and you don't bother to learn to swim past a shitty dog paddle, and then you move to a city o' concrete and skyscrapers and dat's where you learn ta swim? You one crazy *couyon*."

"I had to find something to occupy my mind." I start forward in a beautiful butterfly stroke, but really, that's just to show off. My body hurts too much, and it's too cold, and there are … *things* brushing up against me as I move. I decide to revert to my shitty dog paddle technique.

The frogs are so loud, it's like a damn chorus. There are crickets, and the distant grunting of gators, soothing even as they terrify me. But then I figure, I might look like easy prey, but Phoenix *radiates* a serious do-not-touch-me vibe. Besides that, he's enormous. Codrick, while still taller and bigger than me, was much smaller than his best friend turned brother.

If I were a gator, I would stay away from Phoenix Benoit.

Swimming in this muck is hard work, so for a while, we stay silent, working our way through the swamp until we come up against a dirt road, snaking through the darkness. With me in nothing but a t-shirt and Phoenix nude, I don't quite feel comfortable walking along it, but he climbs out anyway and reaches for my hand.

"Nobody drives this road unless dey live out here, and the only people that live out here are old and don't drive in the dark. Come on, Baby Girl."

"Would you please stop calling me that?" I ask as I take Phoenix's outstretched hand and let him pull me out of the water and onto the bank. Pausing for just a moment, I wring out the water in my t-shirt and take a deep breath. "I told you at the funeral: nobody but Codrick calls me Baby Girl."

"I can't call you *ma moitié,* and I can't call you Baby Girl, so what can I call you?"

"How about my name?" I ask as something large splashes in the water on my right and I jump. Phoenix laughs and shakes his head.

"You a city girl now?" he purrs, his voice far too dark and sensual for our current situation.

"Maybe," I say as slog down the dirt road, my shirt turning into an icy wet sheet in minutes. Fuck. Maybe I would be more comfortable naked?

I keep my eyes straight ahead, on the tree limbs curling menacingly over the road, Spanish moss dripping in fat green chunks. It brushes my head as I pass and I bat

away with shaking my fingers. I just can't decide if I'm shaking because it's cold, because I hurt like hell, because I'm scared, or … because Phoenix's giant bicep keeps rubbing against my arm.

"Mm," he murmurs softly, his eyes heavy and half-lidded, and not just because one of them is swollen and purple from the fight. "I always knew you were tough, but you just proved it out there tonight. You beat a woman who's been working that ring for months."

"So you think I was badass?"

"I think you're crazy. How the fuck did you even think of that plan anyhow?"

I smile as we walk, but it's a tight, sad sort of smile.

"He was going to kill you, you know. That guy, Roch. He wants you dead." I tuck some soggy wet hair behind my ear and then cringe when my fingertips bump against my scalp. "And he doesn't give two shits about his dead sister—if she's really dead, that is."

"You don't think so?" Phoenix grumbles and I shrug, my teeth chattering as the soggy t-shirt bumps against my thighs. It's chafing my nipples, too, which are rock-hard and impossibly sensitive. With a small growl, I yank it over my head and toss it onto the side of the road.

"Well, I'm not sure about the sister, Eliette," I say, crossing my arms over my breasts and finding it impossible not to notice Phoenix's eyes on my naked body. I can feel his body heat radiating out from his massive form, and I can feel his gaze like a laser, skimming my flesh and making my throat tight. "But he hates you. Why?"

"My daddy," Phoenix starts and runs his fingers through his wet violet hair. The motion of those tattooed digits tousling up his wet locks warms me up in ways that I don't want to acknowledge. Don't want to, but can't seem to stop. Denying these things doesn't make them go away.

I'm feeling something for Phoenix Benoit that I ... shouldn't feel.

Two things, actually.

One is primal and feral and wild ... and the other is deep and painful and sensual. It's the second one that scares me the most, and it's the second one I shove as far down inside of me as I can get.

"My daddy," Phoenix repeats after a few minutes of silence, "he slept with Roch's mother, and then his father found out about it ... He was the one that killed my dad in the barfight."

"Roch's father?" I ask and Phoenix nods, exhaling sharply.

"Said it was an accident, but ..." When I look over at him, I can see that his silver eyes are distant and far

away, glassy with emotion. "And then two weeks later, that man's wife had an accident of her own, slipped and fell on a hike with her dogs and drowned in the water." He gestures with is head in the direction of the swamp. "More d'an likely, that man killed his own wife, Roch's, mother. And he blames me for it."

Exhaling sharply, I turn back to the road and walk on in silence.

True to Phoenix's word, nobody drives by or disturbs the quiet, and neither do we. For almost an hour, we stay completely quiet.

"Almost dere," Phoenix whispers as we come to a fork in the road and he leads us to the right. By this time, I'm mostly dry except for my hair, but my thighs are chafing and my muscles are sore and achy. There's a purple bruise spreading across my belly that I can see even in the weak moonlight.

"Almost there in your terms or almost there in mine?" I ask and he chuckles again, the warm, low sound sliding across my skin like hot fingertips.

"Forty-five minutes thereabouts," he says, and I breathe a sigh of relief. "But we'll have to venture off the road and into the water again." I groan but Phoenix bumps me playfully with his shoulder, scalding me with heat. "It's safe out dere, not like at the shop." His eyes darken and I can tell he thinks he made a mistake by letting me stay there. "I'm sorry, Embry—"

I cut him off before he can keep going.

"Please don't apologize. The reason I stayed at the shop was to protect you."

"You protect me?" he grumbles and then he's licking his lips and glancing away sharply, curling his hands into fists. "I'm such a fuckin' *couyon*, getting you dragged into this shit. I shouldn't have let you stay there. It occurred to me, yeah, that they might come looking for me, but not like that. And I didn't think they'd recognize you none or even care. Girls don't have to show back up as long as they keep dere mouths shut."

He rubs a hand over his face.

"Do we have a plan for after we get to the cabin?" I ask and Phoenix gives me this … look that I don't know how to interpret. My breath catches and I glance away sharply.

"What kinda plan you thinkin' about?" he asks me, and his voice is so rumbly and low that I feel this tightening in my lower belly, this primal pull that I could almost swear Phoenix is in control of. He gives a metaphorical tug and my body responds like it's on a string.

"Not that sort of plan," I whisper back, touching my fingers absently to my lips. Phoenix notices and laughs again, that warm easy chuckle that cuts through the night and swirls around me. "I'm not having sex with you."

"We're both naked and wet and aroused and you don't think we gonna fuck?" he asks, stopping in the middle of the road and just staring at me with that heavy-lidded gaze of his. Phoenix's eyes are the color of starlight through clouds, a soft, muted gray that draws me in even when I don't want it to.

"I chose him, not you, Phoenix," I say, and then I hate myself as soon as the words leave my mouth. My stomach clenches tight, and with the extensive bruises, it *hurts*.

"I know dat," he tells me, voice husky and thick. "But I don't care."

"You don't care?" I ask as he gets too close to me, his heat sweeping over my cold form. All I want to do is throw myself into his arms and … shit, I don't know if I want to cry or if I want to have sex or if I want to talk to Codrick. I don't know; I don't fucking know.

"No, I don't," he repeats, cupping my face in both hands. His palms are rough against my skin, but the tex-ture of them is exquisite, lighting up all my nerve end-ings. I want more. My lids slide closed as I struggle to maintain my self-control. "I love you and Codrick both," he whispers, and I can feel his breath against my mouth.

In my mind's eye, I can see him leaning over me, big and muscular and dipped in ink, his bronzed skin shining silver in the moonlight. The swamp is teeming with chirping insects, croaking frogs, hooting owls. All of a sudden, it feels loud out here, impossibly raucous and wild and whimsical, like we're in another world.

"If I have to play second place in your heart, I'm okay with that. He deserves to be number one." Phoenix breathes these words against my lips moments before he kisses me with his whole mouth, parts my lips, tangles our tongues together. My lid's crack open and I can see him watching me with silver eyes hooded in lust, his violet hair hanging over his forehead as he kisses me with a fierceness, a possessiveness that I barely know what to do with.

Phoenix slides one heavy palm down the side of my throat, over the curve of my shoulder, and trails his fingertips down my arm. When he takes control of my hip, I groan into his mouth and fight a sudden rush of betrayal and guilt that does its best to toss water onto this burning ember until it sizzles out.

But ... he's so warm and big and comforting, and even though he was in a fight with blood and sweat,

even though he swam through murky water, he smells delicious. I can't even pinpoint the unique musky scent that clings to his skin, but whatever it is, it makes my nipples hard and my core wet.

Backing up, I feel my feet hit a patch of moss and then Phoenix is dragging me down into the grass, underneath a cypress whose limbs curl over us like a specter's spindly arms.

His huge body is just suddenly there atop mine, his lips kissing down the side of my throat, stubble scraping against my cheek. It feels so goddamn good that all I can do is groan and relax back into the damp earth. *This is weird, Embry,* I tell myself, and maybe it kind of is, but this whole night is weird, and I can't stop the tide of emotion and need that's just washed over me.

My legs open wide and wrap around Phoenix's body, pulling him in against me, so close that I can feel his cock bumping against my slick folds, teasing my clit with a merciless undulation of his hips.

It's been so long since I last had sex that it almost feels surreal. I'd forgotten how goddamn good it felt. *I'm sorry Codrick,* I think, but it's been a long, trying few days and I'm not completely in control of myself around Phoenix. I've always loved him, but … some wires must be getting mixed up in my brain because I'm having trouble remembering exactly what that love was like back then, when we were in our senior year of high school and he would grab me up in a hug so tight that my feet came off the floor …

With another searing kiss, Phoenix thrusts his cock into me and drives those thoughts right out the window. My breath catches and for a moment, it's almost painful. He's huge, and I'm tight, and holy shit. Even though I touch myself pretty regularly, I don't usually do much but stimulate my clit. Since Rick died, it's just been … a bodily function I took care of to relax, not something that felt this fucking good.

And definitely not something emotional.

Holy shit, this is emotional.

Hot tears spring to my eyes as I throw my arms around Phoenix's neck and squeeze him tight, open my mouth and let him take whatever he wants from me. I don't have a lot to give anymore. I'm not a whole person now, and I don't have a whole heart to give.

Phoenix murmurs something soft and in French, right against my lips, and even though I don't understand the words, I can feel them. My lids crack open, and I can see those silver eyes looking right into mine, catching my gaze at the same time he takes my body, fucking me into the dirt with the weight of his massive, muscular form. My fingertips play along the muscles in

his back, trail down his spine, cup his firm ass as he works himself into me.

It's primal and heady, out there in the bayou, naked and alone with adrenaline and danger nipping at our heels.

The man works his hips in those fast, hard undulations that grind my clit between us, even as we start to sweat, our bodies warm from the effort of a good fuck. I know I'm close, at the verge of orgasm even before he puts his right hand on my breast, palms the sensitive mound and rubs the pink point of my nipple between his fingertips.

"I was happy with you bein' Codrick's," he whispers, putting his lips close to my ear as I pant and stare up at the stars, my muscles squeezing and caressing his shaft as my pulse flutters in my throat and my heart thunders. "And I'd give anything to give you back, but I can't." Phoenix stops moving, sliding his hand from my breast to cup the side of my face again. In his eyes, there's an intensity I can't look away from. "I'm just trying to do right by you. I love you, I've always loved you. Now that he's gone, I'm just trying to be there for you because he can't."

I turn my face away and bury it in the crook of Phoenix's shoulder, squeezing him with my thighs and encouraging him to move inside of me while I fight back tears. I can't hear those things. I don't want to hear those things. Because ... emotions are like a river behind a dam. All it takes is one hole, one crack and everything comes tumbling out.

With my eyes squeezed tight, I surrender to the deep, hard thrusts, letting my body obliterate the uncertainty in my mind. She knows what she wants, and she wants Phoenix. Who wouldn't? He's big and beautiful, gentle and strong, charismatic and genuine. But it's *not* Phoenix that's the problem.

It's me.

And my fragile, broken heart.

Fortunately, the climax takes over, bursting through with me in a shuddering wave that tears a small scream from my throat. It echoes around the noisy darkness of the bayou, just another mating sound in a sea of noise.

Phoenix keeps moving, thrusting into my tender heat until he spills himself with this deep, guttural groan of relief. Pumping one last time before he kisses me full on the mouth and then rolls off into the grass on his side.

"I'm big, me," he mumbles against my shoulder with a chuckle, "didn't wanna crush you, no?"

But even though he's cute as fuck, and he's gently biting my shoulder, I'm lying there looking up the stars and trying not to cry because ... because I just don't know.

"We should get going," I say, sitting up and feeling the warm trickle of semen down my thigh. Great. My choices are hop in the water to wash it off ... or deal with it. And I'm not getting back in there with the gators, so I guess I'm dealing.

"You want me to clean you up with my mouth?" Phoenix purrs, wrapping an arm around my tummy and kissing the side of my hip. My body clenches with heat at the suggestion, but ... I can't relax out here. I just need to get inside somewhere and shower and put clothes on, and then maybe I'll feel more like myself.

*Thank God I kept up with the pill.* It helps regulate my oily skin, so even with no boyfriend, no lovers, I haven't stopped using it. As far as ... other adult discussions, those will have to wait until later. I'm sitting naked in a clump of grass next to a gator-filled swamp with the owner of an illegal underground fighting ring chasing after us.

Now is not the time.

"We need to go," I repeat, pushing Phoenix's arm off and rising to my feet.

I start walking before I even see him stand up, and I can tell from the cloud of rage following behind me, that he's seriously pissed.

That's okay though, because I am, too.

Just not at him ... but at myself.

# PHOENIX

## CHAPTER NINE

My Paw-Paw's cabin is buried so far in the untamed murkiness of the bayou that ain't nobody gonna find it without the help of a Benoit boy, and seeing as I'm the last Benoit boy dere is, this is the safest place in the world that I know of.

Embry walks with her arms crossed over her breasts, head tilted slightly down so that her hair hangs forward and covers her face. When I do steal brief glances at her expression, it's steely and closed-off and I got no idea what to make of it.

"You mad at me?" I ask as we walk, dripping from our second swim of the night, along the edge of the island where the cabin sits. This land is owned in trust, under some ol' company name my Paw-Paw made up to avoid the tax man, so I don't see Roch or anybody else finding it.

"I'm not mad," she answers, speaking for the first time since we fucked. Hell, I didn't mean for our first time together to be like that, all messy and weird, ruttin' in da

dirt like gators. Raking my fingers through my hair, I watch Embry carefully, trying to read her body language. Seems damn near impossible right now.

"The sex was no good?" I ask with a cocked brow and a sideways half-smile.

Embry looks over like I'm a stupid motherfucker me, some real stupid git.

"It's not …" she starts, but then glances away sharply, fingers curling into tight fists, locks of wet hair hanging down the sides of her face and against her shoulders and neck. "We both know you know what you're doing, Phoenix."

Throwing my head back, I can't help a laugh. Things might be shit right now, but Embry … Embry makes everything seem … like it ain't so bad after all. I do anything for dis girl, walk on water, wrestle a gator, defy a dangerous underground fighting circuit.

"Must've had a lot of practice," she mumbles and I pause, dropping my head back down to look at her, head tilted slightly to one side as I study that beautiful face o' hers. Even without all the bruising, dere's nothing in the world like Embry LeBlanc. Nothing at all.

A man's heart could gather da strength to beat just from lookin' at her.

"You know how much practice I had," I say, because she was the one that encouraged me to start dating, and then got pissed every time I came back with a story of some girl or another. *I wonder if she was jealous?* But nah, nah. I'm thinking too highly of myself, no? "And I got a lot more while you been gone."

"I don't want to talk about that shit," Embry snaps and I cock an eyebrow, pausing underneath a heavy cypress and giving her a look. "What?" she asks, pausing a few feet ahead of me and glancing back.

"Am I crazy *couyon* or you jealous, Bab— Embry?"

"I'm not jealous, and can we *please* keep going? I need a shower, Phoenix." I look at her, all soggy and wet and naked, and it takes everything I got in me not to turn her around, shove her against a tree, and fuck all dat jealousy right outta her.

"You as beautiful today as you were the night of winter formal," I say and Embry rolls her eyes, this soggy kitten with dark brown hair dripping around her face, bruises all over dat beautiful body, and eyes that glimmer with fire. Even with the dark hair of her cunt showing, those full curves catching the moonlight, she doesn't look scared or embarrassed, just … fierce. "Remember? When Rick got sick, and I took you on my bike? We danced until they kicked us outta dere."

"I don't want to talk about this, Phoenix," she says, breathing hard, trembling. I start to move toward her but

she backs away. "I have moss and probably snakes stuck in my butt crack."

I crack a grin, but Embry just rolls her eyes at me and turns, pulling me along in her wake.

"You don't have any diseases, do you?" she asks, and I shake my head. But she's not lookin' at me, so I pick up the pace to stand beside her, my right arm brushing against her left.

"None, *ma moitié.* Wouldn't do dat to you, me. I get a lot of physicals for dose fights, and I've been tested recently."

"There's a three month window," she murmurs and I grin.

"Yeah, but I get tested every two *weeks*, so we fine, *'tit fille,* relax. I'll get tested again in two more, okay?" I reach up and brush hair away from her forehead, listening to the gentle lapping of the water against the island, and the greedy song of nature all around us.

"Yes, please," she says, dropping her hands unashamedly away from her breasts and turning a look on me. "And you're lucky I'm still on the pill."

"So, lucky, me," I growl back and watch as she shivers in response. After I pause, I just can't help myself. "You been wit' a lot of guys since Codrick?"

"None," she replies promptly, and this deep, possessiveness surges through me. Only Codrick and me ever been wit' Embry. That feels right, like the way it always shoulda been. Fuck. "Don't look so excited about it, okay? Just because we ... whatever that was back there, doesn't mean anything."

"It means everything to me," I say, but then the cabin's in sight and Embry is visibly sagging with relief.

"Thank fuck," she groans as I put out a hand and stop her from moving forward. I *think* we're safe out here, but I won't make a mistake the way I did in the shop. I let her come there, let myself forget the life I'm leading now, and I almost got us into a really bad place. I'll be fucked if I let that happen again.

"Let's check out nice and careful, okay?" I say and she nods, following along behind me as I skirt the edge of the island, past a dock with two old canoes tethered to it. One has a hole and is half sunk, one side perched on the mossy ground of the island while the rest sinks slowly into the deep. The other is new, the one I carved for myself with Paw-Paw's tools. "Stay here," I growl, and then I dart forward onto the back porch and the rocking chairs my grandfather built. He was about a hundred times handier than my dad ever was.

Cupping my hands against the grimy window, I peer inside and find the cabin quiet and dark, just like I left it. The outside might be a little cluttered, with that super special Louisiana vibe, but the inside is nice. I thank

God I had da brains to stock dis place with food and water, gas for the generator, blankets and clothes.

I can take care of Embry the way I should've back when Codrick died. Instead of letting her run off and bury herself in a hole of her own making, I coulda followed her and broken down those walls.

Running my tongue over my lower lip, I banish those memories and step back, moving off the porch and crouching low to grab the shotgun from underneath it. Something crawly slides over my hand as I reach inside, but I ignore it and yank the gun out, brushing off a few spiders and a small lizard.

"You are way too nonchalant about that," Embry whispers from behind me as I glance over at her and watch her eyes tracking a black widow spider's glossy body as it moves over decaying leaves. "The bug, not the gun," she corrects but I just give her a look.

"Didn't I tell you to stay over there?" I growl, but Embry just shrugs, and I let out a sigh. "Alright, fine, come on, girl." Heading around the front of the house, I check the trees carefully. Even cloaked in shadows, I spent enough time in this corner of da swamp as a kid to know what should look like what.

Everything is as it should be so far as I can tell.

Still, I hold dat shotgun as close as I held Embry earlier, and make my way around the entire island, her naked form padding silently along behind me. Once I've cleared it all, I dig up the key next to the front porch and open the door for her. As soon as she sees the interior, her eyes widen and I can tell she's impressed.

"Take dis and wait here while I turn on the generator," I say, but dat stubborn girl follows me out and around the side of the house anyway, staring defiantly as I turn around and glare at her. Probably doesn't help my case none that my cock is rock-hard and pointing right at her. "Nice to see that old spitfire is back," I mutter when I give up on having a stare-down and turn back to start the power. With a whir, the generator kicks to life and we head back inside, flicking on the lights as we go.

"Holy shit, Phoenix," she whispers, staring up the soaring rafters in the ceiling, and then flicking her eyes to the old mason jars strung with lights, the kitchenette in one corner and the bed in the other. There's a small door to the right of it, a tiny bathroom with hot water and a toilet, one of the additions I made to this place by myself in the last year. Embry's father, Devin, inspired me to do it. That, and he let me borrow his tools and his know-how.

"You like it, I take it?" I ask as I take the shotgun from her hands and lie it across the wooden butcher board surface of the counter.

"This is … not what I expected. The last time you brought us out here—"

"It was a dump, no?" I chuckle as I walk over to the wooden chest at the foot of the bed and crack it open, pulling out a thick, fluffy towel and tossing it Embry's way. With a groan not unlike the ones she was making while I fucked her, she dries her hair off and wraps the violet fabric around her body. "I made some improvements, me."

*"Some* improvements?" she asks with a whistle as I tie another purple towel around my hips and head over to the single dresser against the wall. I don't bring girls out here—only ever brought Codrick and Embry period —so it's just my stuff in the drawer. Yanking out a variety of items, I toss them on the bed and cock a brow.

"Take your pick. Shower oughta be ready in a bit." I watch Embry shift through the clean clothes as I pick out my own. She rejects the sweats for a pair of boxers and chooses a purple tank that matches my hair. "You take da first round and I'll start a fire, make us somet'ing to eat."

Dropping my towel, I yank on a pair of jeans and cringe when I have to stuff the hardness of my cock inside the denim. I don't bother with a shirt.

Embry's eyes watch me as I open the door to the wood stove and grab some logs from the stack against the wall. She sits on the edge of the bed, her dark eyes so complex I don't know what to make of 'em. She too smart for me, Embry is.

"We'll lay low here for a few days, and then you gonna get your ass back in your car and head to New York."

"Like fuck I am, Phoenix," she says, standing up and storming across the small space to stand next to me. "I'm not abandoning you, you idiot. Come to New York with me then." Her cheeks flush hot and she glances away, panting.

"I won't drag this trouble along with me, *ma moitié*. That be like dragging a chicken carcass behind your boat and bein' surprised that gators are swimmin' after."

"I'm not leaving you to this shit. We'll figure it out together. I'd bet anything that that creeper guy, Roch or whatever the fuck his name is, has something to do with his sister's death. Either he knows who really did it or maybe he played some part in it himself."

"And how we gonna uncover all dat dirt?" I ask as I shove logs into the fireplace and light it up, closing the door and turning around to look at the only girl I ever loved. Fuck, when I look at her, I can see why she's so set on Codrick being her one and only. When our eyes meet, I know damn sure dere could never be another woman I'd feel this way for.

192

"We'll figure it out. You know these woods like the back of your hand. We'll go back to your place and we'll look for clues."

"They'll be swarming all over dere," I say as I pad over to the kitchen and start pulling cans from a cabinet. Embry moves into the tiny square of kitchenette, so close I can smell her. My tongue flicks across my lower lip again and it takes everything I have inside of me to hold back from grabbing her again. She needs time. I don't wanna spook her, me.

"We'll get in and have a look the same way we got in here. We'll be careful and we'll keep to the swamps. No way those second-rate goons are swimming through gator water to look for us." Embry pauses and exhales sharply. "I know those assholes don't *really* know who I am, but it wouldn't take a hell of a lot of sleuthing to fig-ure it out. I know it's a long shot, but do you—"

"Have a phone?" I finish with a grin, grabbing the satellite phone from the cabinet next to the stove. "Call your parents and tell 'em I say hi."

Embry's cheeks flush with color as she moves away from and heads back to sit on the edge of the bed, talk-ing so quietly I can barely hear what she's saying. Instead, I focus on whipping up some maque chox with what I have in the cupboards. Fortunately, I also got beer *and* a few bottles of wine. My Paw-Paw wasn't a total backwoods motherfucker. He had some fine tastes, that ol' man did.

"They say hi back," Embry tells me, handing over the phone and doing her damnedest to make sure our fingers don't brush. I can't stand it, seeing her naked and wrapped a towel, knowing my seed's still inside of her and yet ... she can barely look at me. "Dad's coming home in a few days. They asked if we could be back by then, but I said I didn't know."

Embry watches as I empty canned corn, dehydrated green bell peppers, onions, dried garlic, and canned tomatoes to a pot and turn it on. There's a jar of bacon grease I saved from last time I cooked breakfast out here and I add a dollop of that, too. Normally maque chox is served as a side dish, but I don't gotta lot of fresh stuff out here. Suppose I could go grab some crawfish, but .. I don't want to leave Embry, not right now.

"You want a glass of wine or a beer?" I ask with raised brows.

"Give me a whole bottle," she says and I chuckle, whipping out one of my Paw Paw's last few bottles of wine that he ever brought out here. I pop the cork and offer it to Embry, my eyes sparkling as I take her in, chugging from the bottle, the perfect pale perfection of her throat working as she swallows. "Holy shit, that's

actually good stuff," she says, glancing at the label before handing it back to me.

"My Paw-Paw was a man with a beer budget *and* beer tastes," I say with a grin, "but my Ma-Maw liked her wine, and he got used to likin' it, too. After she died, I think he took to it because it brought back good memories."

"Poor Paw-Paw," Embry breathes, running her tongue across her lower lip to clean the taste of the wine off. I can't help. Fuck, that gets me.

Stepping forward, I run my tattooed knuckles down the side of Embry's face, and then tuck my fingers under her chin, leaning forward for a kiss that takes my breath away. *Shit, she tastes so damn good, sweeter d'an wine even.* Dis girl here, she's all I've ever truly wanted. Her and Codrick, only parts of my life that were ever worth a damn thing.

"Please stop kissing me," she chokes out, even as her body starts to tremble. Embry swigs another sip of the wine and backs up a few more steps. "It's confusing, Phoenix. I'm … I'm confused."

"What dere to be confused about?" I whisper, trying to be careful but so desperate to be with her I feel like I might choke. "You must know how I feel about you, how I've always felt about you."

"The shower should be ready?" she asks in a strangled voice, taking another swig of wine and then storming off without waiting for my answer. She takes the booze wit' her. With a sigh, I finish cooking and dish up our plates, grabbing another bottle of wine and turning the lights off so that there's nothing but the glow of the fire. Part of me is worried about da smoke, but my rational side knows that there nobody out here wit' us.

It's just me and my best friend's girl.

A while later the bathroom doors open in a rush of steam and there's Embry, all warm and wet, white drifts of heated air rising from her skin. I can feel my cock doin' da same damn thing, thickening inside my jeans until I'm uncomfortable as hell.

"It's all yours," she says, gesturing at the bathroom with her towel and sitting down on the other side of the bed. We look at each other for a really long time, this tense moment that feels like it's stretching into forever. There are so many things I want to say to her, but I don't know if she's ready. Fuck, I don't know if I'm ready yet. How can I be when I got myself into such goddamn trouble?

"Sit and eat wit' me for a minute," I say as she sets her empty wine bottle aside and lays back on the bed with a groan.

"Every part of me hurts," she whispers, cracking one eyelid to look over at me, "even my cunt hurts. You're … big, Phoenix. Bigger than Codrick."

I smile, but it's not smug. I miss Codrick too much for dat although when we were alive, I was merciless in teasin' him about the size o' his dick. It wasn't small either; I'm just hung, me.

"You brought it up," I grumble and Embry opens both eyes, taking the bowl of food into her lap and stirring it with a spoon. "I didn't think you want to acknowledge that we rutted like dogs out dere."

She sighs, and I'm so fuckin' confused by what she's thinking that I just want to chuck my own bowl at da wall and hope that wakes her up enough to explain things to me.

"I don't know how I let that happen," she says, choking on emotion again. It's all stuck up inside her chest and she won't let none of it out. "It's not happening again."

"Embry," I breathe, reaching out to her. But she pulls away, and I find myself gritting my teeth. I want to steal her pain away, rip it out and crush it into pieces, but I can't help her if she won't let me. Hell, maybe we both need help? Maybe we both crazy over Codrick's death? If he could see us now, he'd laugh at our asses and tell us to buck up and move on.

"Let's talk about how to get you out of this mess, okay?" she says, taking a bite of her food and grimacing slightly. I do the same and then frown.

"Damn, this ain't no good," I say but I'm so fuckin' hungry that I down the rest of it in three bites, grinning at Embry as we both show each other our empty bowls at the same time. "A good fight'll do dat to you."

"That place is awful, Phoenix," she whispers, exhaling a low, deep breath and taking both our bowls into the kitchen before coming back to lounge beside me. There's nowhere else to sit or I imagine she'd have taken that spot instead. When she gets close to me, I see her nipples pebble and her thighs shift restlessly inside my boxers. "Next time they put you in the cage, it's going to be to the death."

"I figure that much," I say, grabbing the second bottle of wine and drinking deeply from it. I pass it over to Embry and she clutches it in two hands. "I've never seen one of those matches but … there's big money riding on them. They'll put me in there and they'll want me to kill a few people before they set me up to be killed myself."

"So we find out what this Roch really knows or maybe even did to his sister and then … they'll let you go?" She turns to look at me, but I don't know the answer to that. My daddy owed a lot of money, but I paid a lot of it off, too. Would they hunt me down in a

different city? Now, the answer is yes. But if I cleared my name or exposed Roch, then ... maybe I could leave this place and start somet'ing new with Embry?

"That would do the trick," I reply, leaning back into the pillows and feeling two nights of rounds in the ring rushing back at me. Plus the swim, plus ... my first time bein' inside of Embry and it's too much.

Even though I plan on ravaging her ... I fall fast asleep instead and I dream of Codrick.

In dat dream, he's as sure as I am that Embry and I are meant to be together.

Even a ghost knows as well as I do ... that dis is fate.

# EMBRY

## CHAPTER TEN

When I wake up, I have no idea where I am or who I'm with, what time it is or what the fuck is going on. Sitting up with a gasp, I find Phoenix lying beside me, still snoring and looking ... horribly adorable with his violet hair falling across his brow. His stubble is nice and thick today, a layer of blonde over his tanned skin.

Without thinking, I reach out and rub my knuckles against his cheek.

Surprisingly, he doesn't stir and I continue with my exploration, running my thumb against his lower lip and trying not to think too hard about last night, about his huge body on top of mine, pushing into me, filling me up and dragging me over the precipice of pleasure. It felt so good, almost too good.

I felt like I was betraying Codrick the whole time.

Pulling my hand away, I stand up and explore the small cabin. There's not much to it, so after a while, I head outside and just sit on the back porch with a warm beer I

snaked from the cabinet. According to the satellite phone I peeked at before coming out here, it's almost four o'clock in the afternoon.

We slept late, me and Phoenix.

Then again, we sort of deserved it.

With the shotgun across my lap and the sun playing over my bare toes, I feel a brief moment of contentment, like I'm safe here. Like I could stay here forever and nothing bad would happen to me ever again. It's all an illusion, that much I know, but it feels good. It's exciting to sit behind someone else's or something else's walls instead of my own.

"You shoulda woke me, you," Phoenix says, ruffling my hair and yawning at the same time. He's showered now, reeking of my mother's mint soap as well as that special husky spiciness that always clings to his skin—whether he's drenched in blood and sweat from a fight or freshly showered and dressed in clean clothes.

My body has an instant reaction to that smell too, my nipples pebbling and my heart pounding away inside my chest.

"You needed the sleep," I say as he sits down beside me and I'm glad to see that I'm not the only person here with a swollen eyelid and a puffy lower lip. But whereas I'm moving stiff and slow, Phoenix glides around and sinks into his chair with fluid, muscular grace. My throat gets tight but I glance away and out at the water, the yellow sunshine reflecting off the surface and making the woody marsh sparkle. "So, what do we do now?"

"We wait," he says, getting out a pack of cigarettes from his jeans pocket and lighting one up with a lighter from the other. "Just hang out and enjoy da scenery." Phoenix lifts his head up to exhale and I find myself mesmerized by the white smoke dancing over his lips.

For a while, we really do just sit there enjoying the silence.

"You want to catch some crawfish?" he asks eventually and I glance over, trying not to look too closely at that *RIP CODRICK* tattoo. "It's not exactly the season, but they a pest and they everywhere anyway. And then maybe we can eat better tonight."

A smile teases the edges of my lips and I try really fucking hard *not* to think of fishing for crawfish with Rick and Phoenix on a boat in the middle of the night, the stars and moon as company. Still ... it sounds almost ... fun? I haven't had fun in forever.

As I watch Phoenix rise to his feet in a fluid motion, his tight t-shirt rising up and flashing the flat expanse of his lower abs, I wonder if I'd have fun doing *anything* if he were around?

"I've missed you," I choke out, even though words that would be innocent yesterday suddenly seem so ...

personal. Intimate. Devastating. My heart clenches with pain and I glance away sharply. "I missed you from the moment I left town."

There's a long pause, so long that I'm forced to look back to find Phoenix staring right at me, tall and broad, casting a long shadow over the porch. His hair looks even more purple in the afternoon light, his lips extra full and pink, his tattoos twice as bright. The red tent draws my attention and holds it because I'm too much of a coward to look into those beautiful gray eyes.

"I miss you, too," he says, his voice gruff and thick. For such a strong, imposing man to have that look about him … it makes me almost certain that I could bring him to his knees if I wanted. "I miss you every second, and I don't ever stop thinking of you. Never. You on my mind every damn day." He taps the side of his head with two fingers and then moves away to dig through a metal box next to the house, pulling out some rods and setting them on the ground next to the brown boots he's wearing. "They more active at night, but we can try and catch some now. You wanna take da boat out?"

"Sure," I breathe, and I mean to get up and go inside to grab some beer and snacks, but all I can really do is replay those words over and over again inside my mind. *You on my mind every damn day.* Blinking rapidly, I force myself to my feet, shoving my arm across my eyes to pretend like I don't feel any tears coming.

Phoenix is dragging them out of me.

Four hundred and whatever the fuck days and *now* I'm crying?

But it's not just Codrick that I'm crying for.

It's me.

And ... it's Phoenix.

---

Our little boat ride is one of the best things that's happened to me since ... prom night. It's easy and relaxing, and I don't have to try with Phoenix the way I do with everyone else. He gets me without my having to explain. That, and ... I can actually talk about Codrick. I find myself laughing over stories that for months have been making me throw up. Just a single thought straying to them would make me physically ill.

But not right now, not with Phoenix Benoit and his big gruff laugh that shakes the whole boat, arm muscles rippling as he drags another crawdad into the boat and traps the lobster-like creature under a crate with several others.

We'll eat well tonight, that's for sure.

"I didn't think running for my life would be so … fun," I say with a loose shrug, watching a heron take off from a nearby branch and spread its wings in the dying yellow and orange rays of the sun.

"Yeah, well, I know how to entertain the ladies, me," Phoenix says with a sly half-smile. All his smirk serves to do is make me hot and bothered inside, the soreness between my thighs calling out for more of him. I feel like I was given a sample, and I want the whole damn thing. I'm sold. Sold on Phoenix Avit Benoit.

"Is that sexual innuendo?" I ask as he adjusts his big frame, making the boat rock and sway rhythmically beneath us. There are so many things I want to say to him, so many unspoken truths that need to be said.

First off … I owe him an apology. I ran away when he needed me most and I'll never forgive myself for that. There's not excuse; no matter how I was feeling, I should've put him first. He put me first those first few days after Codrick's death. Hell, he put me first those first few *minutes*.

Second … well, I'm not ready to think that far ahead.

"Maybe," he hedges, a roguish smile teasing his mouth as he pulls another crawfish into the boat and tucks it under the crate. He's caught like ten while I've caught … two. Must be that magic Cajun touch.

Phoenix lifts his gray eyes to mine.

"What would you think if it were?" he asks and I shrug. *I'm a traitor; I betrayed Codrick,* my mind wails, but I don't believe that, not really. Not on the inside where it counts. Deep down in there, I know that me and Phoenix being together ... would only bring him joy. Fuck, if he's looking down on us right now, he's probably cursing up a storm because of how stupid we're acting.

"You're just a friend," I say, but the words are hollow and there's no strength behind them. My eyes stare into Phoenix's, trapped there by the intensity of his gaze. There's so much emotion riding in this stormy irises, swirling around, desperate to come out. I bet there are a lot of things he wants to say to me, too. "Or maybe ... maybe you never were?" I ask, thinking about how much I craved his hugs, about the sparks between us when we touched, the way he looked at me sometimes ...

Phoenix sighs and closes his eyes, listening to the sounds of the bayou. He says his favorite part are the splashes, unknown animals sliding into the water. He enjoys the mystery. I hear one of this big plops from somewhere nearby, smiling and shivering at the same time; I hope it's not a snake.

There are, like tree snakes everywhere out here. One fell on my back earlier and I let out a very undignified scream.

"My soul was split in two pieces," he tells me, attaching another worm to his line and dropping it into the water. We're floating right next to the shore; the boats even attached to a nearby tree with a length of rope, but it makes it more fun somehow than sitting on the island. That, and we paddled around earlier, just for fun. "One belonged to you and one to Codrick. He was … my brother in spirit."

Phoenix leans back and then runs his fingers through his violet hair. The tattoos on his hands dance in the light from the lantern sitting in the boat between us, casting strange shadows. It's gotten dark while we've sat out here, and I don't even care. I'm warm inside my borrowed sweater and happy that it smells like mint and musk and spice.

"When Rick died," Phoenix continues, his eyes shimmering with far away memories, "I took that piece and I gave it to you." He focuses through the shine of nostalgia and my heart stutters in my chest. "I was always in love with you, *mouche a mielle*, but I would never o' done anything to break you and Codrick up, no."

He scrubs a hand over his face and my breath catches.

Why does he have to be so goddamn beautiful? The muscles in his arms ripple with each move he makes, and the lavender tank he's wearing stretching across the impressive width of his chest. That strange sex we had last night has only made it worse, this painful ache inside of me.

"I'm not a whole person anymore," I say aloud, echoing my thoughts from last. There's a tug on my line and I yank it up, but there's no crawfish—just a missing worm.

"Too quick dere, girl," Phoenix says, reaching out and hooking a new worm to my line. He rinses his hands in the water, dries them on his jeans, and then reaches out to take my hands, his thumbs moving over my knuckles in a way that draws the breath out of me and makes me shudder. "Nice and slow. Nice and slow," he murmurs, looking right at me and drawing goose bumps from my flesh.

"Did you hear me?" I ask, and all of a sudden, I'm fighting back tears. A whole year and a third and I didn't cry. And now Phoenix has made me cry, what, three times? Asshole. But being here with him, I feel things opening up inside of me, springing to life. Seeds long dormant and dead are now blooming bright. He makes

me feel human, Phoenix does. "I don't have a whole heart to give you."

"Dat's okay, *ma moitié*," Phoenix says, rubbing his thumb in soothing motions. "Whatever shape your heart is, mine's shaped the same way," he repeats. "We both broke that day and we never put ourselves back together, me and you. We both still fragmented and … bleeding. We both *en d'oeuille*—in mourning—Baby Girl."

The name slips out of him and he pauses, cursing under his breath in French.

My insides twist together and I glance away, but this time, I don't yank my hand from his grasp. This time, I don't fight it.

"I'm sorry I ran away from you," I say, and my head feels detached from the rest of my body, like I'm floating over this scene and looking down. "The day of the funeral; I'm sorry I ran away when you called me Baby Girl." The words choke out, like knives shredding my throat and tongue as I speak.

But I don't care.

It doesn't matter.

They *have* to be said.

"I always loved you as … Well, it doesn't matter how. I just loved you with my whole heart, just like I loved Codrick. You needed me and I left, and I left you behind and—"

Phoenix leans forward, knocking over the lantern and making the boat sway, and he kisses me on the mouth with a possessive heat that steals my breath away, makes me surrender to this wash of both pain and healing that's taking over like a summer storm.

He kisses me until our groans punctuate the quiet dark, blend in with the insects and the frogs, the ripples and the splashes.

After a moment, he breaks away and *jumps* out of the boat, landing in the shallow water with a splash. Phoenix unties the rope and drags me back to the dock, tying us up again before he reaches in and scoops me up and into his arms.

"Phoenix," I start, but my heart is pounding so quick. I'm sweaty and confused and … I want this. And there's no reason why I shouldn't want this, right? All of my fears from last night wash over me in a wave. Guilt, that sick sense of betrayal … and then the awful fear that maybe soul mates really are once in a lifetime.

Because … because I like Phoenix. I do. I love him, even. There was always something hot and wicked between us, but I didn't acknowledge it because I had something special with Codrick, too. And if I'm perfectly honest with myself, I'm equally scared of finding out that either of them *isn't* really my true love.

Fuck.

That's it right there, in a nutshell.

I'm as scared of finding out that Phoenix *is* my soul mate as I am of finding out that Codrick wasn't. But no, no, that's all bullshit. I *always* loved them both, and love isn't a pie to carve up right? It's a well, deep and always wet, overflowing and endless.

"I'm scared," I tell Phoenix, burying my face in the crook of his neck and shoulder. "Of you, for you, of this stupid situation. If I hadn't left you, you wouldn't be in it."

"Not your fault, Embry," he whispers, and I just suddenly want to hear him call me anything but. I realize I'm hypocritical, that I *just* chastised him for doing what I now crave with an intensity that's making me sick. "*I* got me in dis mess and *I* will get me outta it."

"With *my* help," I chastise, exhaling sharply as he kicks the door open and then heels it shut behind him. He's even got enough strength to briefly let go of me to lock the damn thing.

Phoenix chuckles and the sound reverberates through his entire body, making my bones quiver and shake. I love it. I love that ... and I love the sound of his heart, thrumming softly against his ribs. It's strong and steady and sure.

He tosses me down on the bed, making me bounce slightly before he reaches down and flicks the button of his jeans.

"Did you hear me, asshole?" I ask and he laughs again, shaking his head and then shoving the denim down his hips to expose the erect length of his cock.

"I hear you," he tells me, making his way back to the light switch and plunging us into darkness. He grabs a second lantern off the counter though and brings it over, switching it on and setting on the side table next to the bed before he takes off his shirt. I can see all of him now, in the soft light.

His body is toned and hard, covered in ink and faint scars from that stupid motorcycle accident. He's thick and ready for me, his erection proud and almost intimidatingly large. My thighs clench together as a warm heat takes over my core, making my muscles clench and flutter. Last night ... he was so good last night, and I couldn't enjoy it.

If I'm going to do this now ... I will. I want to.

"You can call me whatever you want," I breathe as Phoenix climbs on the edge of the bed and looks down at me with those brilliant eyes of his, like thunderclouds, fierce and sharp and loud. "Because ..." I choke as Phoenix lies down beside me and puts his big hand on the back of my head. He pulls me close and presses our

foreheads together. "You're all I have left of Codrick, and if you call me Baby Girl then … it's almost like I can hear the echo of his voice again."

Tears come *again,* but Phoenix just brushes one away with a rough thumb.

"We'll get through this together, Baby Girl," he says and now that I've decided not to fight it, it feels so damn good. So fucking goddamn good. "I want to live with Codrick inside my heart for the rest of my life, me." He touches a big palm to his bare chest and lay my fingers over his head, squeezing it tight. "But I won't live with this pain. We heal it *together.*"

"What's happening right now?" I ask, because I'm too scared to put a name to it.

"You talk too much," Phoenix replies, his voice thick and hoarse and lazy with sex. Before I can get another word out, he's pushing his mouth up against mine and kissing me hard, sweeping his tongue across my lower lip and invading my mouth with all of that vibrant heat. When he kisses me, I feel things shifting inside of me, making room for … feelings. And well, let's be honest, the long thickness of his shaft.

Reaching out a hand, I tickle my fingers lightly along the length of him, finding the tip wet with a pearl of pre-cum. Slicking my palm over the head of his cock, I'm pleased when he thrusts his hips against me.

We explore each other's mouths with a kiss that's so intense that I'm sure Codrick can feel it wherever he is, these ripples of emotion that we're sending out. If we could see his ghost right now, he'd probably tip his head back and laugh, clap his hands together and throw up a mighty prayer.

*"You two are perfect for each other. Shit, what were you waiting for all this time?"* That's what he'd say. And then he'd smile, look into my eyes one last time ... and disappear.

"Fuck, I've missed you," Phoenix whispers against my mouth, his words rumbling through me as he kisses me with barely restrained passion and heat. It feels like he's going to break if he holds back anymore. One of his big, warm hands is resting on my hip, squeezing tight as I stroke him with a hard, firm grip. His penis is hot under my palms, quivering slightly. It's clear that he wants me and that he wants me *now.*

Emotion coils in my chest, tight and achy, and I find myself shoving down the boxer shorts and the sweats I dressed in for the boat ride, kicking them off my ankles and rolling onto my back.

Phoenix comes with me, his heavy weight crushing me into the bed as I part my knees and switch my hands to his back, dragging my nails over his muscles again. This time though, I won't let myself be guilty. No, this

time, I'm going to embrace this moment. Phoenix is all that's left of the heart I had before the accident, the one that was whole and pure, bright-red and beating. He's a fragment of that, a walking talking remnant of who I once was, made up of my love and Codrick's love … but also, just a genuine human being.

Even completely separate from Rick, I would've liked him.

With both hands, Phoenix pushes up my tank top and exposes my breasts, squeezing one and separating his mouth from mine to suck the peaked hardness of my nipple. He braces his left hand against the headboard and then drops his right to my hip.

Our eyes meet in the lantern light just before he drives into me, making my head fall back as he fucks with violent thrusts, these deep, hard movements of his hips that fill me completely, stretch me apart and stroke every sensitive place inside of me. Phoenix isn't rough, but he's determined and persistent, fucking me until his body tenses, the hardness of his muscles straining against his skin and dotted with sweat.

As soon as he finishes, shuddering above me, the sounds from his throat so deep and guttural that I almost come, too, he rolls off and tucks me against him, reaching his hand between my thighs and teasing my swollen clit.

"You aren't gettin' any sleep tonight, bumble bee," he whispers, licking the shell of my ear and running his tongue down the sweaty side of my throat. "No sleep."

A shaky moan is all that I can manage with Phoenix's hot hard body pressed to my back. I can feel the coarseness of his leg hair against my own smooth thighs and calves, the soft sound of Cajun French purring in my ear. He rubs my clit with surprisingly gently motions considering his size, playing with it without touching any of the too sensitive nerve endings directly.

"What you got so far is just a taste," he continues, slipping two fingers inside my wetness and using his own cum as lube to fuck me slow and deep with his long, tattooed fingers. His thumb finds my clit again, teasing it with gentle swirls until my back arches and I reach my hands down to stop him.

"That's good enough," I choke out because I can't take it anymore, being teased to climax with that big beautiful hand of his. "Too much," I gasp, but Phoenix has me locked in a tight grip, refusing to let go until I clamp down around his fingers and arch my back, pushing my ass into him and groaning a curse into the quiet air of the cabin.

"That's good, Baby Girl," he murmurs, sucking and biting my ear again. "Come for me." And I do, shuddering and shaking and gasping.

Phoenix removes his fingers from inside of me and cups my cunt tightly, giving the plumpness of it a squeeze as he kisses the side of my throat.

"You know what this means?" he whispers, but I can't talk. Too many emotions. Too much pleasure. My eyes sparkle with tears, but I blink them away because fuck them, I've cried enough tonight.

"No," I manage to scrape out past a throat hoarse and raw from my frantic groaning.

"It means you mine now. You belong to Phoenix Benoit."

"Get over yourself," I choke out, but all he does is laugh and squeeze my pussy again. It feels so fucking good that I forget to be angry. Shit, Phoenix is the kind of guy who's impossible to be angry *with*.

"Codrick woulda willed you to me and we both know it," he continues and instead of getting upset, I laugh. I actually *laugh* at the mention of our dead soul mate.

Our.

Because really, that's what he was. Ours. *We* lost him. *We* suffered, didn't we?

"You're a dick," I say, but that's really not what I mean and the softness of my voice betrays me.

"You like me, yeah?" he asks and I feel my cheeks flushing. "I know you *love* me, but you like me, too? You want me to be your man?"

"You're ridiculous," I sputter as he slides his hand to my hip and uses that strength of his to push me so that I'm lying on my back and looking up into the dark depths of his eyes.

"I love you," he says and the starkness of his words makes my entire body flush hot. I find my pulse racing, my head swimming with a dizzy sort of contentment that I haven't felt in … four hundred and nineteen days. "I always have. And I was okay with you not being mine before. But now? Shit, now dat I've seen you again? I gotta make you mine."

Phoenix sweeps hair off of my forehead and looks at me with this simple intensity that says he knows exactly what he wants. I find myself licking my lips and shifting to be closer to him.

"I do like you," I say, reaching a hand up to play with the blonde stubble on the side of his face. I love that, the pale color of it paired with his violet hair and tan skin. He looks fierce and wild, untamable. "And I've always loved you."

Phoenix smiles, a soft expression on the hardness of his face, and then he moves down and away from me, pushing my knees apart and grinning. The way the

lantern is casting light, all I can see in that moment are his eyes and his teeth. He looks fierce as hell.

"I told you weren't done yet," he whispers, dropping down and putting his face between my thighs. With a gasp, I reach up and curl my fingers around the top of the headboard, holding on for dear life as Phoenix rubs his stubbled face against the softness of my thighs, before he starts to kiss and lick. I writhe beneath his touch as he clamps down on my hips with two big hands and flicks his tongue along the swollen length of my folds.

I know he's tasting that mix of his seed and my own wetness, and it turns me on like crazy. Before he's even really gotten *started*, I'm moaning and thrusting my hips up to meet his face. Well, I try anyway. He keeps me locked down tight, sucking and kissing and caressing the outer folds before he dips his tongue in deep and swirls it around my opening.

Sweat pours off of me as Phoenix works my body with this almost agonizingly slowness, taking his sweet time, torturing me with the rough stubble on his cheeks, the slick heat of his tongue, the gentle pressure of his lips as he kisses my clit.

Without warning, he slips his tongue between my folds and swirls it around the sensitive pink nub, white hot pleasure fracturing and breaking behind my lids.

Even when I reach my hands down and fist them in his hair, he doesn't stop. He keeps going, ratcheting the intensity up to a point where I feel like I might climax again.

"I'm coming," I groan out … right before the bastard pulls away. "What are doing?!" I ask as he chuckles and slides off the end of the bed, grabbing my ankles and pulling me to him. I have no idea how long we've been going at it, but he's hard again, nice and thick and still slick from my juices.

"You gonna come again, don't worry, Baby Girl," he says, looking right at me with those big gray eyes of his. Phoenix pulls me all the way to the edge of the bed and then pulls me to my feet, putting one hand behind my head and kissing me silly. "Now turn around."

Biting my lower lip, I do as he says and let him push me over the end of the bed. My feet catch on the decorative bottom slat of the footboard, giving me the perfect amount of extra height needed …

Phoenix curls his left hand around my hip and caresses my ass with his right, giving the pale flesh a squeeze with his inked fingers. I bury my face into the blankets and exhale, hoping I don't come the second he thrusts into me. It feels like I might.

Using his foot, Phoenix teases my legs further apart and then slicks his already lubed cock between my folds,

teasing my clit with gentle thrusts of his hips. Strange sounds escape my throat, as my body responds with a rush of heat to my core. I'm empty and I want to be filled—*now.*

"You're making me not like you as much," I growl out after the teasing turns into torture. Phoenix has the audacity to chuckle at me right before he lines himself up with that throbbing emptiness and *fills* it.

A groan explodes from my throat and I press my ass back into him, taking him balls-deep as he plunges in with long, slow strokes. He's so big that I'm riding that edge of pleasure and pain, but it doesn't last long. As soon as I tilt my hips up and into him, it's just fucking right.

It's fucking perfect..

Phoenix is fucking perfect.

"Can you make love to me?" I whisper, the sound so quiet I'm surprised he hears me at all. But he does; he stops moving and slides out of me, turning me over with a gentle hand on my hip and helping me sit up on the edge of the bed before stepping between my thighs.

"You smell and taste like honey," he whispers, just before I wrap my legs around him and he slips inside of me again. My arms curl around his neck and he kisses me nice and deep and long, filling with me easy, sure strokes in the lantern light.

This time, he makes sure that I come first, tightening around him and biting his lower lip as the climax sweeps over me with a wave of emotion that brings tears to my eyes.

Phoenix finishes inside of me and then we just sit there and hold each other for so long that I start to wonder if the sun is going to come up sometime soon.

"I got something for you," he says, sliding out of me and bracketing my face between his big, warm hands. He kisses me one more time and moves away, grabbing something from the pantry and bringing it back to me, his beautiful inked body glistening with sweat as he moves. "This is exactly what *you* make of it, you hear me?"

I raise an eyebrow as he lifts a can of mixed nuts into the light, pops the plastic white top and then reaches out for my hand, forcing me to hold it palm up.

"You wait right dere," he says, licking his lower lip and then turning the can over into my palm.

My eyes fill with tears at the same moment my heart fills with both pain and love.

Because right there in the palm of my hand is Codrick's ring that I left on the windowsill four hundred and nineteen days ago.

# PHOENIX
## CHAPTER ELEVEN

"Somethin' ate dem crawfish last night," I say with a wide grin, leaning in the cabin doorway and watching Embry as she pulls on a pair of sweats like she hurtin'. "Either dat or they run away on their own," I add with a chuckle, teasing my fingertips along my own arm.

Embry stands up and gives me this lopsided little smile, the ring sparkling from her finger. I don't know what she wants to make of it, and I don't care. Codrick gave it to her and she has a right to have it back. But if she wants to be my life, well, I ain't gonna complain about that either. Oh, fuck no. Last night was no joke; I'm her man now and that's that.

I'm never lettin' go of dat girl again.

Never.

"I hurt you last night?" I ask as she makes her way stiffly over to me and then crosses her arms defiantly over that black tank she borrowed. It swims on her and there's a lot of side boob action, but I'm not complainin'.

"I fought in a ring just like you," she says, lifting up her shirt to show me the bruises on her belly. "But you're a man, so you think everything revolves around your giant dick, I get it."

"You sore then?" I ask, my grin stretching from ear to ear. I haven't felt this good in over a year, me. Not since Codrick died. Not since Embry disappeared. My little bumble bee. "I'll be more gentle next time."

"How long are we staying here?" she asks, rocking back and forth slightly on her feet. She's anxious, dat's for sure. "I mean, I like it out here, but I also don't want to just sit around and wait for Roch to find us."

"He never findin' us out here," I say, glancing over my shoulder at the swamp. She don't take kindly to outsiders. Flicking my attention back to Embry, I do my best to give her some space. She made big strides last night, and if I scare her off, I'll never forgive myself. "But you're right. I got a shop to sell, a house to rent out, and a life in da big city to plan."

"You'll be miserable there," Embry says, her eyes focused on everything *but* Ol' Phoenix over here. Stepping forward, I turn her face back to mine and get lost in those dark eyes. Fuck me, I could look at 'em all damn day. "You'll hate the city."

"If I'm wit' you, then I'm happy. That's all I need."

"So you say until you're being woken at three in the morning by an ambulance, or until reality sets it in and you have to get a job there. You'll hate it, Phoenix." I frown at her, but I'm not swayed. She couldn't get me to leave her side if she told me we were movin' to da fuckin' moon.

"Let me worry about what I hate or don't hate," I mutter, leaning down to give her a kiss. As soon as our lips touch, she melts into my arms, putting her small hands on my chest and makin' me feel ... fuckin' possessive as hell. She's *mine* and I'm not going nowhere. "You like the city?" I ask, breaking the kiss but letting my lips hover over hers. My cock thickens inside my pants at the feel of her breath on my mouth.

"It's ... big and anonymous, impersonal and gray and crowded and cold." Embry pulls away from me and puts her face in her hands. "I made myself like it because it was *nothing* like home and for a long time, I wanted to be anywhere but here. But I hate it, Phoenix. I fucking hate it. I hate everything about living there." I reach over and pull her hands away from her face, dragging her toward me and wrapping her up in my arms. Resting my chin on the top of Embry's shiny dark hair, I let out a long sigh. "If we'd moved there together like we planned, me and you and Codrick, we'd have stayed a week before turning around and coming right back."

"Then stay here," I whisper, and she stiffens in my arms. "The memories are dere no matter where you go, *ma moitié*. Being here, it doesn't make it worse. Only thing that makes it worse is *not* being wit' you."

Embry stays quiet for a long, long time, but she doesn't make any move to pull away from me.

"I missed your hugs," she whispers after a while, and I feel myself smiling against her hair.

"I missed holding you." That earns me as small chuckle before she puts her palms on my chest to get some space between us.

"All that aside, we *need* to figure out this thing with Roch. I can't start a future with you if I'm worried something is going to come crawling after to bite us in the ass."

"Start a future?" I ask and her cheeks flush as she shoves away from me and heads over to a row of shoes against the far wall. They're all monstrous on her, but what I can say? I got big feet … and big other t'ings, me. "I like the sound of dat."

"And I like the sound of you *not* dying," she says, shoving her feet into a pair of sneakers and bending down to tie the laces as tight as she can. "So grab the satellite phone, let's get in the boat, and let's find out who the fuck killed Eliette."

There's no real easy way around out here. No, Mother Nature does her best to be confusing as hell. Good thing I got directional sense, me. Also, good thing both Embry and I got muscles, because there are several spots where we gotta drag the boat over small strips of land or through shallow water. Airboat would be nice, but too loud. I ain't got one anyhow.

"We go on foot from here," I tell her as we climb out one last time and drag the boat onto land, hiding it behind some bushes. It's already startin' to get dark which is perfect because I know dis place like the back o' my hand. I've lived here my whole damn life, so whatever Roch got planned, he won't get da jump on me when I'm ankle-deep in muck. "Engine's too loud, but we gotta swim one last time."

Embry stifles a groan as she trails along behind me, weaving through the thick, tangled limbs of cypress trees and over to the long, deep channel that runs along the back of my house. We got a dock there, too, but I won't risk us bringing the boat up to it.

"Get on my back this time," I argue, but once again, Embry dives into the water and starts to swim. I curse in French for a moment before following after, swimming slowly and quietly down the narrow channel until I see the back porch light shining faintly. It's always on when I'm awake and off when I sleep because I hate havin' it glare into my bedroom window.

"Did you leave that on when you left?" Embry asks, and I nod, treading water and searching the quiet darkness of the trees around us for any sign that Roch's men are waiting.

Everything looks alright, but with Embry, I won't take a single damn chance.

Instead, I swim a ways back and help her out of the water at a marshy embankment just far enough away that the porchlight is a speck in the distance. We wring out our clothes, and then I take one of her small hands in mine, grasp it tight and start weaving my way around the back of da house.

The going is slow and slippery; poor Embry falls to her ass three times before we make the half-circle around the back and end up close to the dirt road that comes into the property.

"I don't see nobody out here, but there's always the chance they're in da house," I whisper, studying the empty driveway and wondering if there's a trap set for me in there somewhere.

"Let me call my parents," Embry says, and I dig into the pocket of my soggy jeans for the satellite phone. It's waterproof, but we stuffed into a plastic bag just in case. "Everything seemed fine when I called, and we don't have any reason to believe that Roch actually knows who I am." She makes the call, and then speaks quietly to whoever's on the other end. After about thirty seconds, she hangs up and turns to me with a nod.

"I called my mom's cell; they're at the hospital to pick Dad up. They should be home in a few hours at most. Nothing seemed amiss though." She shrugs loosely. "You want to try going back to my parents' place? We can change clothes and regroup."

"Let's try Priya's place first," I say and Embry raises her eyebrows at me. "Don't get jealous, you," I whisper, reaching out to tuck thick, dark strands of wet hair behind her ear. "There ain't nothing between us, that I promise you."

"But you've fucked her?" she asks and I chuckle, pulling her close to plant a kiss on her forehead.

"Wear dat jealousy more often, looks good on you, Baby Girl." We both pause at the sound of that nickname sliding past my lips. It feels good to say it, like it's been trapped inside of me for far too long. Every fucking time those words leave my lips, I hear an echo of Codrick. Makes me feel like he's here with us somehow. "No, Priya and I don't fuck. It's strictly business." I grin and reach down to grab Embry's hand again. "But she got a car, and she's a helluva lot closer than your parents' house."

We start moving again, side by side, walking through the trees with nothing but my instincts to guide us. If my Pa hadn't been a drunk, I might not've played out here so much and I might not know my way right now. Maybe a blessing in disguise, dat?

"Have you dated a lot of girls since high school," Embry whispers as we walk and I smile softly.

"No, I didn't date any," I whisper back, but we know what she's talkin' about. "I fucked a lot. I don't know how many. I didn't care." Embry's fingers tighten around mine, and I grin. "But I won't be touching another woman as long as I live; the one I wanted came back to me."

"I still don't ... know what's going to happen, Phoenix. I'm still processing." I smirk and glance away because dis girl, she don't know what she just got herself into.

We keep walking, almost four whole miles to Priya's trailer. When we get here, I scope out the place but I

don't see nothing and the trailer is dark. Her car sits in the muddy driveway, right where she always parks it.

I turn to Embry and put my hands on her shoulders.

"You stay here and if somethin' happens to me," I start, but she reaches out and slaps her hand over my mouth. The distant sound of male laughter echoes through the trees and we both pause, turning to watch the house until the front door opens and someone comes out.

A sigh of relief escapes me as I see Priya wrapping her arms around the guy's neck and kissing him on the mouth. She leaves him to sit in a rocking chair on the porch just before she disappears inside and comes out wit' two beers, the silver cans shimmering under the porchlight.

"You still stayin' here," I growl, but Embry wraps her arms around mine and gives me a hard look. "Do I gotta tie you to a tree to get you to listen?"

"If you had rope with you, I might be scared, but you don't," she says snootily, and I roll my eyes. But at the same time, I'm bursting with joy in the inside just to have her here wit' me.

"Fuck," I curse, but everything seems okay, so I drag her along with me, out of the trees and onto the hard-packed dirt and water-filled potholes of the driveway. "Hey!" I call out and both Priya and her date

231

jump. When we get a little closer, I realize I recognize that guy as a waiter from that restaurant Embry and I had pancakes at. "What you doin' up so late?"

"Jesus Christ, Phoenix, you scared me!" she scolds as I bring Embry into the circle of yellow light cast by the porch lamp. There's one of dem mosquito zappers there, too, flickering and buzzing as insides get too close and die an awful fuckin' death. Assholes. I'm sure by now I'm *covered* in bites. "What the hell are you doing? Taking a midnight stroll through the goddamn swamp? And by the way, thanks for calling and leaving a *message* to tell you'd be gone for two days. I had to call in that part-time guy to do some of your appointments and the clients were *pissed*."

"Family problems," I mutter because I'm not about to get into this with yet another person who doesn't need to be involved. "I need to borrow your car. Just for one night."

"I can't lend you my car," she says, gesturing at her date as if to say *he ain't got no way home*.

"Have a taxi come out here and get you both in the morning and I'll reimburse you later. Both Embry and I left our keys at the shop; you take your pick of a ride until we get your car back to you."

Priya comes over to the edge of the railing and leans her arms against the splintered wood while her date sips his beer and looks annoyed at having his evening of fun interrupted. Bet he thought he was gonna get some out here on da porch.

"Why did you guys leave your shit at the shop? Her purse was there, your wallet. And you didn't bother to lock up. You're lucky we didn't get robbed, Phoenix."

"I'm a bit distracted me," I say, lifting up Embry's hand in explanation, the engagement ring glinting brightly, like a fuckin' star come down to earth.

"You're getting married?!" she practically shrieks, and then flashes me a bright grin. I flick my gaze down to Embry's and see her cheeks flushed pink. I don't really know if dat's the case—I didn't exactly ask her after all—but the lie works and Priya slaps her palms down on the railing. "*Fine*, even though it's a huge inconvenience"—pause for dramatic eye roll—"I'll let you borrow my car. One sec."

Priya heads inside and comes back out with a set of keys, tossing them down to us with a smile.

"And congratulations on getting married. The second I saw you two together in the shop, I knew it was meant to be."

■ ■ ■ ■ ■ ■ ■ ■ ■ ■ ■ ■

Embry drives us back to her place—I know how she feels about cars and fuck, I don't blame her none—passing by the house three separate times before she actually pulls into the driveway and parks. We climb out and pause at the bottom of the single porch step while Embry tries to find the spare key.

"They moved it after Annamae's divorce," I say, smiling in amusement and heading over to a rusted old wheelbarrow with Noelie's succulent garden planted in it. The key is tucked against one side, so I dig it out, carefully not to disturb any of the tiny plants, and pass it over.

My fingers brush Embry's and heat rushes through my body, giving me a painful erection that hurts ten times worse for bein' inside these wet jeans. We stare at each other for a moment before she shakes her head like it's need clearing, and heads up to the front door, unlocking it and leading me down the hallway to the closet and grabbing a couple fresh towels.

"You could borrow some of my dad's clothes," Embry starts, drying her hair off with rough motions of the towel against her scalp. She pauses all of a sudden and sucks in a deep breath. "Or we could get you some of Codrick's clothes if there are any left in the bins? I know you took his stuff, but … I had a lot of things

buried in mine." Embry closes her eyes, her pulse jumping as her hands start to tremble.

Tossing my towel aside, I grab both her hands in my own, forcing her to drop her own towel as I bring her fingers to my lips for a kiss. As soon as my lips brush her skin, she stops shaking.

"I didn't touch any of your bins," I promise, softly, "but I'm more than happy to wear Devin's clothes."

"No," she breathes, shaking her head like this is suddenly the most important thing in the world. "No, let's … I'd feel better if you were wearing his stuff, like maybe he'll see you more clearly and help us get out of this mess."

I smile, but it's a sad one and reach out to cup the side of her face.

"You want to change into some dry clothes first?" I ask, but she shakes her head and pulls away from me, heading back down the hallway like she's on a mission or something. I follow after her, pausing when she stops to grab a flashlight from a kitchen drawer, and outside, to the barn and up the ladder. There's a blue tarp in the back corner and when we pull it aside, disturbing all sorts of creepy crawlies, there's a heap of plastic bins with lids.

Embry collapses to her knees as I put my back to the wall and slide down, pulling her into my arms for several long, quiet moments before she starts to cry, quiet and soft, the sound muffled against my shoulder. Whispering to her French, I stroke her hair back and row her slowly, fighting back tears myself.

Love and loss, those are like strings, and they find us like nothin' else, wrap us tight together in a little cocoon … one dat we don't break out of until morning.

# EMBRY

## CHAPTER TWELVE

Sleeping in baggy, wet clothes isn't fun, but even with the cool night breeze, I'm warm tucked in Phoenix's massive inked arms. The way he holds me reminds me of everything that's good in the world, all the things I loved—*love*—about Codrick. But also, it reminds me that Phoenix is special, too, always has been, always will be.

"My parents are probably freaking out right now," I say as I push up from his chest and glance into sleepy, heavy-lidded eyes. Phoenix gives me a gentle half-smile as I sit up and yawn, stretching my arms above my head and listening to the soft patter of rain on the barn roof.

"Jorie came in here last night hollering for you, and I told her to fuck off." My eyebrows fly up to my hair-line, and I can't help but let out a small, choked laugh. The idea of *anyone* telling my older sister to fuck off is priceless, but gentle giant Phoenix? Wow, I almost wish he'd woken me up to see that. But then ... there was something therapeutic about sleeping here next to my old life, packed up neatly in plastic bins. Something inside of me gapes open as I stare at it and suddenly, I just want to rip all the lids off and tear it apart until it's as messy as my emotions are.

"Breakfast should be fun," I say with a smile, licking my lower lip and forcing my quivering hands over to the first bin to pop the lid. I can't help but notice the engagement ring as I do, my thoughts straying once again to Codrick and the life we should've led.

"Dey all left together to pick up your dad's prescriptions and get some supplies for breakfast. They tried to keep Devin in bed, but you know how dat ol' man is." My smile gets a little more real as I set the lid aside and start digging through my sweatpants and hoodies. Sure enough, I find both a pair of pants *and* a top for Phoenix within *seconds*. That's how entangled my life was with Codrick's, wrapped up into a tight little ball, inexorably joined together.

Yanking them free, I fight the urge to smell them and pass them straight into Phoenix's hands. He catches my fingers as I do and gives them another kiss, just like he did last night. Surprisingly, that actually works to calm me down a little.

"I don't know what's going to happen after this," I whisper as I notice the hard edge of a book peeking out from the clothes. I know right away what it is: Codrick's yearbook. "But—" My breath catches as Phoenix releases my hand and I lean forward, snatching the book to my chest and holding it tight as I turn to look into those beautiful silver eyes of his. "I want to take all of this stuff to your place and go through it with you."

"You got it, bumble bee," he murmurs softly as I put the bin's lid back on and cover it with the tarp. Phoenix and I rise to our feet and exchange a long, quiet look. Fuck. Now that I'm here—the last place in the world I ever wanted to be—I don't want to leave. I hate New York. I can see the appeal for others, but it's just not for me. It's not what I want.

"Can you teach me to tattoo?" I ask on a whim and Phoenix laughs, reaching out with one to ruffle my hair as he holds Codrick's clothes reverently against his chest with the other.

"Whatever you want, I'll do it. Anything except leave you or let you leave." He winks at me and I pretend not to be affected. But I am, down to the deepest, darkest shadows of me. It feels like tiny, concentrated beams of sunshine are penetrating all the way down, breaking me into pieces, ripping me apart. But in a good way. I'm tired of living under my own personal storm cloud.

Phoenix is … my sunshine.

Cheeks flushed with pink, I make my way down the ladder before he can get a read on my expression, enjoying the feeling of him shadowing me as we head across the yard and into the unlocked house. Fuck, my parents need to be more careful … I should probably warn them, but the thing is, I have no idea what to say. If I mention one word about what's really going on, they'll call the cops and I'm not sure the local police are trustworthy. I've never liked any of 'em before.

We just need to figure this shit out—and *quick*.

"I'm gonna shower," I tell Phoenix when we reach the end of the hallway, standing between the door to the den and the one to the bathroom. I set the yearbook on the small decorative table against the wall before glancing over at Phoenix. The look he gives me is *priceless*.

"There room enough in there for two?" he asks with a wicked smirk, and I find myself biting my lip again, shifting slightly as the soreness—yes, the asshole really did make me sore—reminds me how exquisite it is to have Phoenix between my thighs. I wonder if Codrick had lived … if we'd had ever ended up in a threesome? There were those few times where he encouraged us to

kiss … Maybe he noticed something between me and Phoenix that I was too dense to get?

"You're huge," I tell him and his smirk gets even dark and more mischievous. "More than just your dick," I say with an eyeroll, but all he does is laugh and push me into the bathroom. "You better lock that door because if Jorie finds us in here …"

"Jorie's always been an unfair bitch to you," Phoenix says as I start the shower and he very purposefully flicks off the lights. There are no windows in here —just this crazy high-powered fan my dad got to fight the moisture problem—so it's pitch-black. My heart pounds as I quickly shove my still damp sweats to the floor and rip off my borrowed tank.

My plan is to scramble into the shower and—

Phoenix gets to me first, wrapping his arms around my waist and kissing down the side of my neck. As soon as he touches me, I give up any pretense of fighting him. I don't want to. Fuck, the only thing I've wanted besides the sweet kiss of death since Codrick's crash is Phoenix Benoit.

"I won't let her bully you anymore," he growls against my ear. At the same time, he lifts his right hand up and cups my breast, kneading the tender flesh with strong, firm fingers. "She never believed in you and Codrick, so clearly, she's a damn *couyon*. I never liked her none." Phoenix bites my earlobe and then makes this purely male sound under his breath that has my whole body heating to a boiling point. "Now get in dat steam and let me get you dirty before I clean you up."

He lets go of me and I almost fall over, weak at the knees and practically swooning.

Ugh.

Thank God it's dark in here or I might never live this moment down.

Pushing the shower curtain back, I climb into the hot water and groan, sinking underneath it and scrubbing what I think is *mud* from my butt crack. Oh God. There's a reason people don't regularly swim in swamps.

Phoenix steps in next to me and even though he's way too fucking big to be in here with me—hell, he'd hardly fit even by himself—I love the hot heat of his presence. He radiates all of these … *feelings* that I've been running from for so long, emotions that make me feel alive and real and more than just a shattered, broken mess of a human being.

"We should hurry before my parents get home," I whisper, and even though I'm nineteen and used to living away from home, the thought excites me.

"Short and quick," Phoenix grumbles, scooping my wet hair back and … washing it? Oh shit, he's washing

my hair for me. Exhaling sharply, I force myself to stand still as goose bumps break out across my skin and I reap some sort of strange erotic pleasure from having my scalp massaged. "I can do that, me."

"You better do that because even if Dad's not feeling well enough to kick your ass, Jorie just might." Phoenix chuckles and gently pushes me forward so that my hair is directly under the water, rinsing the soap away as I sigh in pleasure.

"I was thinking …" he starts, his voice distant and far away, like there's something he knows he should say, but is too distracted to properly give a crap about it. "Tonight, we go to Roch's place and scope it out. We won't get too close, but a drive-by shouldn't hurt. Don't know what we'll see, but it's a start."

"I like that idea," I whisper as he Phoenix conditions my hair with those big warm hands of his, digging his fingertips into my scalp in a way that makes me feel almost literally insane. How can something feel this amazing?!

"You know what I like even better?" he purrs after he rinses my hair for the second time. "The idea of fucking you in dis shower right here."

Phoenix puts his hand on my back and gently pushes me over, forcing me to put my palms against the shower wall as he takes hold of my hip with tight fingers. If my dad hadn't insisted on the extra-long bathtub so that he could take his soaks, we'd have never fit in here. But I'm pretty damn certain he never expected me to be doing this in his bathroom.

Curving a hand under my left thigh, he lifts my leg up and helps me position a foot on the side of the bathtub, giving him full, uninterrupted access to that throbbing ache between my legs. Positioning himself at my swollen folds, Phoenix carefully pushes into me. At first, I'm a little worried about lubrication—the shower usually washes it all away and makes shower sex a little *eh* for my tastes—but fuck, Phoenix Avit Benoit must really do it for me because I'm slick as hell and he slides right in.

This low, primal sound escapes my throat as he buries himself all the way to the hilt, breathing some ridiculously sexy sounding praises in French before he starts fucking me. Our bodies move together with wet-sounding slaps that I can't help but like, even as I'm slightly embarrassed by them, and I find myself surrendering to the pleasure, to Phoenix and his big hands, to the connection between us. It feels like I'm falling, but like I have someone just waiting to catch me.

My breasts swing as he thrusts into me, slow at first and then harder, faster, until we're both moaning like crazy and my body does what comes naturally, soothing

Phoenix's cock with hard, fast pulses. I sneak my left hand to my clit and rub in tight, quick circles, matching his pace as he comes hard enough to *growl*, burying his dick balls-deep as I finish up and nearly collapse from the force of my climax.

It's … just about that moment when the bathroom door is kicked in and the shower curtain is ripped open.

Goddamn fucking Jorie.

---

"You think being engaged excuses that sort of behavior?" Jorie scoffs as we all sit around the breakfast table and I try to decide if I'm more embarrassed or … happy? Am I happy? At least for one brief, little moment there I am.

"It does in my eyes," my mother says, coughing slightly from embarrassment. She carefully plays with the scrambled eggs on her plate and casts sidelong glances at my father. He hasn't stopped glaring at Phoenix since we sat down for breakfast, but at least Annamae's stopped giggling. Jorie, though, has been a whirlwind as usual. "They might not be married *yet*," she continues, eyeing my ring with a certain amount of respect. She knows it's Codrick's, of course—everyone at this table does—but they're all smart enough not to mention that. "But we should've seen this one coming."

Mom's mouth twitches in a way that makes me narrow my eyes.

I have the strangest feeling in my gut, like she *planned* for me and Phoenix to get together. *Huh. That's probably why she kept inviting him over, isn't it?*

Also, I know we're not *really* engaged, but ... how stupid would I be to think that won't happen someday? It will. After all we've been through together—not only in the last week but throughout our entire lives—it feels like destiny. I've known Phoenix forever, loved him forever. Only two minutes separates my first meeting with Codrick and my first meeting with him. I wonder if their introductions had been reversed if things would've turned out differently? Not that I'd ever stop loving Codrick. I will love him until the day I fucking die, but ... I think I love him and Phoenix equally? Maybe I always have?

Or maybe the big, handsome Cajun idiot just screwed me senseless in the shower and I'm not thinking clearly?

"Well, if they're getting married ..." Dad chokes out, but even though he just had a heart attack, he kind of looks like he wants to strangle Phoenix. I imagine that if my new 'fiancé' hadn't been spending so much

time out here making himself a part of the family, that my dad might've grabbed the shotgun by now. "Just … make it official so your conservative old father can die in peace," he coughs out as I roll my eyes and pretend like Phoenix hasn't just reached under the table to squeeze my knee.

"I'll make this right, me," he declares, reaching his right hand up to ruffle the damp violet strands of his hair. "I'll give *ma moitié* whatever wedding she wants."

"This *is* the twenty-first century," Annamae says, surprising me as she glances across the surface of the table and meets my eyes. "People don't have to be married to have sex."

"You live in the south," my mother says, pretending to give her a stern sort of look, "start actin' like it."

"Well, I think it's an egregious affront," Jorie says, glaring at Phoenix. I raise my eyebrows at her because, really, she's being a cunt *just* for the fucking sake of it. She goes through boyfriends like paper plates, uses them and casts them aside.

"Look," I say, putting my fork down and holding my hands up, palms out in surrender, "I won't tell Mom and Dad about that time I caught you in bed with two football players if you'll stop complaining about me and Phoenix." I pause and pretend to grimace as Jorie's mouth drops open and both my parents turn to look at her in shock. "Oops?"

Jorie's cheeks flush red as she stabs a sausage and puts it to her lips.

"You sure you don't want *two* sausages?" Phoenix asks, and even though I try to hold it back, a laugh escapes me, so loud and raucous that it startles almost everyone at that table but him. I think ... Phoenix might've been one of the only ones who ever thought I *could* laugh again.

"Well, if you're happy ..." Jorie grumbles, biting the end off the meat while glaring pointedly at Phoenix. "Then I guess it's fine. Just ... don't let me ever hear you moaning like that again; I'm bound to have night-mares."

■ ■ ■ ■ ■ ■ ■ ■ ■ ■ ■ ■

Phoenix and I spend the rest of the day with my family, and even though spending time with them reminds me of Codrick—he was basically the son they never had—I can see that Phoenix fits in the same way he always has. Better, maybe, than he used to. I think maybe my mother's finally forgiving him for the cigarette burns in the carpet—but maybe only because it's finally been replaced with hardwood floors.

"You sure you want to do this?" Phoenix asks as I drive past the spot where it happened. I don't slow down, don't get out and cry. Almost. But then I think about where I'm going and what I'm doing, what Codrick would think. He *definitely* would not want me out in the rain, on my knees in the gravel, reliving that horrific fucking moment when my world changed forever.

No, he'd much rather I kept driving, my hand resting on the yearbook tucked between the two seats. Phoenix's hand rests over mine, keeping it warm.

"I want to," I whisper, throat tight, voice hoarse. I could maybe cry again, but then, I'm already sore between the thighs and I'd rather not have a sore throat and sandpaper dry eyes to go along with it. "If I see her then I think I'll have taken another step. You've basically pushed me down a set of stairs this week, so I may as well go along with it."

"Push you *over* is what you mean," Phoenix purrs, and my skin ripples with pleasure at the sound of his voice. Of course he'd take my metaphor and turn it into sexual innuendo. He's been a smug male since I let him mount me on the ground like an animal. My mouth twitches into a slight smile, helping to banish some of the pain in my heart.

Am I going to be over Codrick if I do this, if I take this yearbook to his mom's house and say hi?

Fuck no.

I will *never* be over Codrick. When it comes to grief, there is no magical solution, no button to press or pill to take or path to follow to find some sort of final, ultimate ending to the pain. Sometimes, the pain *never* stops, but learning to live with it—really *live* and not just survive—is something I can think I can do. Especially with Phoenix. After all, he's in the same boat I am. We loved Codrick; we lost him. And we share almost all of the same, beautiful memories.

I don't even have to think to get to the Landry's place. I've driven there so many times in my life, I could probably crawl blindfolded to it from any direction, scale mountains or swim rivers, and I'd still find my way no problem.

The sun is just starting to go down, and all the lights are on, cheerful and pleasant, as warm and inviting as I remember it.

"Fuck," I whisper as I pull up out front and just sit there for a moment with Phoenix, the car's engine ticking and cooling as I take long, heavy breaths. Glancing over at him, I see that he's got a similar expression on his face.

"You can do this, Baby Girl," he says, reaching over and stealing a rogue tear from the corner of my eyelid with is thumb. "You got this, and I'm right here wit' you. I promise Mrs. Landry don't bite as bad as she used to."

"Will she hate me for stirring up old memories?" I ask, flipping Codrick's yearbook open and running my fingers across the hopeful, happy messages. He was liked—*loved*—by a lot of people. Now, my yearbook, the one where he scrawled out the most beautiful proposal in the whole fucking world, that's mine to keep forever. But this? Maybe it'll bring his mother some sort of peace. Her, and me.

"Nah," Phoenix says, his voice low and soothing, an easy rumble that makes my lids fall closed and my heart beat wildly inside my chest. He has both a calming *and* exciting effect on me. It's weird; I'm not even sure how to explain it. I feel like I could cuddle up in his arms and fall asleep as easily as I could drag a fistful of his purple hair and yank him close for a kiss. "We have lunch every once in a while and we talk about Codrick."

"Really?" I ask as I open my eyes. Phoenix nods and gives me a lopsided smile that almost makes me forget what we're planning on doing *after* this. Scouting out some psycho's house. I should be scared, but I'm not. Just like I climbed in that ring and kicked an opponent's ass for him, I know I'd do anything. Whatever it takes. Well, except stay at my parents' house like he asked me to. Fuck that.

We're not going to suffer alone anymore; this is a joint thing now.

"So let's go before they think we some crazy stalkers and *Mr.* Landry comes out here swinging that baseball bat o' his." Phoenix winks at me and opens his car door, reminding me that we've been sitting in the driveway for a long time. In a town this small, people can get weird about stuff like that.

As we're making our way to the front door, it opens and Codrick's mother is standing there with a giant belly, swollen and pregnant, her hand resting lightly across it. That makes me stop for a minute. I literally just stand there on the grass and stare at her. Once upon a time, *Codrick* was in that belly. And now …

Fuck.

Phoenix grabs my hand as I blink past another surge of emotion, forcing my feet across the lawn and over to the cement steps of the front stoop.

"Mrs. Landry," I say and her smile says it all—she missed me. Even if she *was* kind of a bitch to me when her son was alive, the emotion on her face is genuine.

"Oh, Embry," she says, and then she's leaning down and pulling me into a hug that's full of so much warmth, so many old memories that I can barely breathe. Choking back more tears—fucking Phoenix opened the floodgates apparently—I step out of her embrace and then hold up the yearbook. "What brings you all the way down here?" she asks as she takes it from me and turns it over, her eyes misting as she glances at the cover, running a single finger over the embossed gold words.

"I'm in town to visit my dad," I say and she nods like she's already heard the gossip. Even if Phoenix hasn't told her about my father's heart attack, somebody else is bound to have already done it. "And I thought you ... might want this."

Flipping it open, she studies the words carefully, the wind tousling her dark hair around her face. As I watch her read all the messages from Codrick's friends—I took pictures of them with my phone before bringing it over here because I'm selfish like that—I wonder if being pregnant is helping her cope. Either way, I'm not judging but I barely survived losing a friend and a lover, and I have no idea how horrible it must be to lose a son.

"Do you want to come in and have dinner?" she asks, lifting her face up and struggling to hold back tears. "Nothing fancy but chicken and vegetables with some biscuits ..."

"We'll have to take you up on dat offer next time," Phoenix says, this warm, comforting presence on my right side. He lifts up my hand and shows her the ring, the one she didn't want Codrick to buy for me—with his own money, mind you—the one she threw a massive fit about when she found out that we were engaged. "But dis girl and I, we might not be going far," he says, glancing over at me.

Obviously, the decision to change schools and move back here is *huge* but I don't want to be in New York anymore. And it's not because of Phoenix because I believe him when he says he'd come with me. No, it's so much more than that. It's the sound of the frogs and the crickets; it's the stupid swamp; it's my parents and my sisters and Codrick's mother.

She studies the ring for a long moment before tucking the yearbook against her chest and smiling at us.

"I'll hold ya to that then," she says with a small sigh, her eyes still watery and far away with memories. I wonder if she's going to cry when we leave, but even if she does, I won't judge her for it. "I always thought you two had a thing," she adds, pausing as she turns back toward the house and wagging a finger at us. "Codrick used to laugh when I brought it up, but I saw it. It was there all along."

I raise my eyebrow as she gives us a little wave and disappears inside, closing the door softly behind her.

# Baby Girl

"Still a bit of a bitch?" I whisper and Phoenix chuckles, pulling me into him and giving me a small, quick kiss on the forehead, this hot brush of lips that turns me on in ways that are totally inappropriate given the situation.

We're about to stalk the bad guy.

And sex and bad guy stalking … they don't really go hand in hand, do they?

255

# PHOENIX

## CHAPTER THIRTEEN

That douchebag Roch lives in a pretentious mini-mansion on the edge of town, not all dat far from the fucking warehouse and all the shit that goes down dere. He fights people to the death in dat ring—to the *death*—and all for sport and money.

He's the epitome of everything that I hate.

"Do you think he could've killed his own sister?" Embry muses, slowing down as we pass the house. I know for a *fact* there's a big death match tonight. Alotta money gonna be ridin' on dat fight, so Roch'll be out and about somewhere. If he's already at the warehouse, I'll be surprised. Asshole likes to make an entrance and always comes late.

"A man who watches people kill each other wit' their bare hands? No doubt in my mind." I exhale as we leave sight of the house, head up the road a ways and pull over. If we drive past Roch's house again too soon, one of his dumb shit goons might see us.

Embry parks and turns to face me, tucking her knee up on the bench seat of Priya's old Chevy Impala. My bike and her car are still parked at the shop. Well, dat or Priya's taken them by now. It's not safe to go to back for dem just yet.

"How long should we sit here before we go back?" she asks, her dark brown eyes focused on mine. I can't stop staring at the smooth line of her throat, the full lush curve of her lower lip. And fuck me, those breasts underneath the tight black t-shirt she's wearing? It takes some serious effort on my part to tear my gaze away. By the time I do, I glance up to see *her* eyes locked on the hard bulge in my jeans.

"How long you want to wait?" I ask, the car tucked behind a thick stand of trees in the driveway of a fore-closed house, dark and shuttered away from the world.

Embry swallows hard and raises her face to mine.

"Here?" she ask, but … why da hell not?

Reaching long, inked fingers down, I unbutton my jeans and free the thick hardness of my cock. Without prompting, dat girl surprises me, getting on her knees on the bench seat and leaning down, tucking long silky strands of hair behind her ear.

She flicks her eyes back up to mine just before she takes the head of my cock between her lips, her tongue darting out and teasing the bead of pre-ejac from the tip.

*Holy motherfucking hell.* Leaning my head back against the passenger side window, I drop one hand down to her hair and massage her scalp with gentle fingers.

My eyes feel heavy and half-lidded as she takes me into her mouth, sucking and swirling her tongue around my dick, her ass up in the air as she works me with slow up and down movements. Those beautiful lips of hers tease my shaft, forcing me to breath in short, hot pants. The windows are fogged up in minutes.

"Right dere, bumblebee," I whisper as she reaches out with one hand carefully cups my balls, giving them a squeeze at the same time she increases the pressure of her mouth. "Right dere is fuckin' perfect."

Embry works me into a frenzy with her lips, her tongue, her hand, and then she pulls back, breathing hot breath against my wet shaft and kissing her way along the underside. She moves her hand to the base and gives it a squeeze before replacing her mouth.

Relaxing back into the seat, I let all dose sensations roll over me, sweep through my body in hot waves. My fingers tighten in her hair as she increase her pace, drawing up an orgasm straight from my balls and into the head of my cock.

"I'm real close," I growl out, warning her. But she doesn't stop, keeps her mouth on me, licking and sucking, scraping her teeth every so gently against me.

Squeezing a fistful of her hair, I thrust my hips up and come hard in her mouth, panting and cursing in French as she takes it all and then sits back, swallowing and running her tongue across the shiny pinkness of her lower lip. "Jesus Christ, Baby Girl," I growl out and she grins.

"Good way to kill time, right?" she says, sliding back into the driver's seat and starting the car while I button up my jeans and smirk at her.

"You a fuckin' goddess, you," I tell her and she smiles, pulling around the circular driveway and heading back in the direction we came. As we pass Roch's house again, I keep my eyes peeled, doin' my damned best to ignore the wet throbbing heat in my cock. Fuck, I could go again so easy ... Maybe if we don't see anyt'ing on dis round, we— "Shit."

The word explodes from me, fierce and wild.

"What?" Embry asks, flicking her eyes to the left for just a split-second. I don't know if she's able to tell as easy as I am what I'm seeing out there, my eyes locked onto a figure in a pale pink dress, big blonde curls bouncing around her shoulders as she heads from the double front doors of the house to stand next to a man smoking a cigarette. "Phoenix, what is it?" she repeats as I blink several times and lick my lower lip.

"I just seen a dead girl," I whisper as we turn the corner and head back in the direction of Donaldsonville.

■ ▨ ■ ▨ ■ ▨ ■ ▨ ■ ▨ ■ ▨ ■

"Eliette is *alive*?" Embry chokes out, shaking her head and blinking several times in rapid succession. "Why? How? What the fuck would Roch gain by pretending his sister is dead?"

Staring at the knee of Codrick's old holey jeans—they're a little tight, but I make do—I put together pieces in my head, make up a puzzle that I don't much like lookin' at.

"Fuck," I growl, raking my fingers through my hair and turning to look at Embry. Her face is lit from the blue lights of the dashboard, giving her a seraphic glow dat's actually real appropriate considering she's my angel. Having her back here, it's both a blessing and a curse. I want her so bad, but I wish I was the one to chase after her. Dat, and I don't like her gettin' tangled up in my mess, me. "He wants me to fight in a death match," I whisper because it makes so much sense that way. "Roch tells me he'll kill me for what I done to his sister *or* I fight for him. He knows I'll win. *Shit.*" I lean my head back against the seat. "Either dat or he want a reason to convince his Dad and the other big

rollers in dere to have a reason to force me into a match I don't wanna do. If he tells everyone I hurt Eliette, then they'll drag me in dere kickin' and screamin' and they won't think twice about it."

Embry takes a deep breath in, hold it, and then lets it out slowly.

"So what do we do?" she says, glancing over at me. "If Eliette isn't really dead, I doubt they'll want to play along with this charade for very long. What if ... we went back to New York? Even if we don't want to stay there forever, I have a place and a life set up there while we plan something else. With Eliette alive, they won't have any reason to chase after you, not for some stupid ploy. If we disappear, they'll move on, right?"

I snap my fingers and turn to face her, still wearing my seat belt of course. Embry wouldn't start the damn thing otherwise and I don't blame 'er.

"That's fuckin' brilliant. When did you get so damn smart?" I ask and she smiles, eyes focused on the road, hands carefully tightened around the wheel at two and ten. "They know I didn't hurt nobody, so once they realize I'm gone, they'll forget about Ol' Phoenix."

"You are pretty forgettable," she hedges as I smirk at her.

"Yeah, well, you pretty forgettable yourself, *mouche a mielle*," I joke, rubbing my right hand up and down my left arm and grinning. "I don't remember nothin' about you except your favorite color, your favorite food, your birthday, and that sexy little black dress you wore the first day of junior year."

"You're ridiculous," she says as our headlights sweep the darkness outside. "What's the plan then? We go back to your place and pack ..."

I'm already shaking my head.

"Too risky. No, maybe we just drop Priya's car off and grab whatever vehicle she left dere and we go." I tousle my hair as I try to think of a way out of this without stopping back by the shop. It's too risky, but all our money is there—her purse and my wallet. And this isn't our car. We gotta make a quick stop. "I'll call Priya and tell her to grab our stuff from inside the shop and meet us a few miles away. We won't get very far without any money."

I give a tight smile and make the call. Lucky for me, Priya picks up on the first ring and agrees to meet us about halfway. Good. We don't gotta stop at my place or Embry's parents or anything at all. We'll get our shit and we'll go, and when this has all blown over, we can come back if we want. Or maybe not. I don't even care so long as I'm with *ma moitié.*

We make the rest of the drive in tense silence, pulling over next to Priya along an empty stretch of street, all the shops closed up for the night. Doesn't matter though because the streetlamps are bright as hell and there's a white security truck ambling along down one side of the road.

"Finally, I get my car back," Priya groans as we park and climb out, taking our purse and wallet—minus a few bucks for dat taxi—and handing over her keys. "You kids drive safe now, you hear?" she says with a small, waving the jangling ring our way.

"Do you think she'll watch over the shop for you?" Embry asks as my receptionist climbs into her car, buckles up, and drives off down the empty street, past the security truck and then to a red light that seems to last forever.

I turn my gaze back to Embry and brush some hair off of her forehead.

"I know she will," I say as slowly, almost reluctantly, she passes over the keys to her car.

"I wouldn't let anyone in the world drive me," she starts, hazarding a small smile. "Nobody but you, Phoenix." I return her smile, give her a quick kiss on the mouth and then gesture at the vehicle with a nod of my chin.

"We best get the hell out of here, no?" I ask as the white security truck pauses beside us and a man with a gun steps out. When I go for my own gun—I mighta

borrowed one or two from Embry's dad's collection—
the man simply shrugs his shoulders and lowers his own.

"Roch'll be here in a minute," he says, this smug ass
expression on his stupid fuck face. "You might want to
hear what he has to say about that girl's family. Embry
LeBlanc, right?"

Embry's face pales as the man leans his back against
the side of the truck and waits. In just a few seconds,
another car—a long, sleek one—pulls up and Roch steps
out, smiling tightly at me.

"I'm getting fucking sick of having to track you
down," he says, nostrils flaring as he tucks his hands
into his pockets and flicks his oily gaze between me and
Embry. When he looks at her, I feel this possessive rage
sweep over me. He touches her and I'll fucking kill
him. "Finding this girl," he says, pointing his finger at
her, "was goddamn easy. This town is way too frigging
small." Roch smirks at us, giving the handgun clutched
in my grip a casual glance before redirecting his attention to my face. "That, and I thought I recognized her
from something. She's that long-lost love of yours, eh,
Phoenix?"

"Eliette's alive, so what the fuck do you want from
me?" I snap, gritting my teeth as I lower the weapon and
try to figure out what the hell I'm supposed to do here.

Roch knows who Embry is … which means he knows who and where her family is, too.

*Fuck.*

"I *want* you to put the gun down and get your asses in this car right here," Roch says, pointing at the leather seat behind him. "And then I want to take you back to the warehouse where you're going to fight in a match and you're going to win me ten times as much as you earned last time. You live through it and well, you can have your girlfriend back." Roch steps aside, like he's waiting for us to climb into the car. "Or you can refuse and we can have a firefight right here and now. And then the men I have waiting down the street can go in and kill all four people in the LeBlanc house. When they're done with that, maybe I'll send them down to the Landrys' place and see what havoc they can wreak there."

Slipping my hand into my pocket, I pull my phone out just enough that I can glance down and see the screen. One quick tap of my thumb sends a call straight to Priya. But that's about all I can do with Roch starin' at me like that.

"You fuckin' *couyon,*" I curse, gritting my teeth tight and glancing down at Embry. She looks right back at me, but what choices we got right now? All crap, dat's what. If I fight though … there really is a chance that

Roch leaves her alone because he'll want me to *keep* fighting. How long I don't know, and what'll happen to Embry if I lose ...

But I won't lose.

I'll win her every time, me.

"Phoenix," she says, but the tightness of her voice tells me she doesn't know what else to do. I never killed a man before, but if ... if that's what I gotta do to save my girl, I'll do it. Better than her or her family or Codrick's pregnant mama gettin' shot tonight.

Fuck, fuck, fuck.

"Alright," I say as I set da gun down on the hood of da car. "Let's go. I'll fight for you, but if I win, you let this girl go and you keep me, you understand?"

"You're not exactly in a position to be making demands, you fucking stupid coon-ass, but get in the car, win me some money, and I'll see what I can do."

More than anything, I want to put my hands on either side of Embry's face and kiss her sweet mouth, tell her with my lips all the things I'm feelin' for her in dat moment. But I can't and won't let Roch see exactly how much she means to me. If I kiss her now, even a heartless, soulless sack o' trash like that motherfucker would know that this girl, she means the whole world to me.

# EMBRY

## CHAPTER FOURTEEN

Once again, I find myself at the back of the huge, heaving crowd, sweat pouring down the sides of my face and back, soaking the armpits of my t-shirt. Not only is it hot as hell in here, but I'm freaking the fuck out. Phoenix *can* win; I know he can. He's one tough ass motherfucker.

But to kill some random guy? For no reason other than some rich asshole wants to win *more* goddamn money? It'll break his soul to pieces, crush his spirit. I can't let that happen and yet, I can't see a way out of this either.

I don't know what to do.

Phoenix stands in the ring, the bright lights shining on his violet hair, turning it a brilliant shade of purple. My thumb plays across the band of the ring—it's almost *their* ring to me at this point, Codrick's *and* Phoenix's—as a second man is led up the stairs and into the cage.

He's as calm as Phoenix, this detached but determined look on his face.

I wonder what dirt they're holding over him? Because I don't know many men that would risk their lives with odds like this, *especially* not for the measly payout that's funneled down to the actual fighters. In the other matches—like the one I participated in—it was a pittance, an insult really. Now? It's a joke. A fucking goddamn joke and everyone here ... is sick in the head.

The women in bikinis do their thing with the signs; the man with the microphone does his.

And then Phoenix and his opponent are crouching, circling one another with slow, careful steps. This fight is much less hurried than the previous ones I witnessed. Not surprising since lives are literally on the line.

My throat is dry and my stomach is clenching with nerves, but I've got an armed guard on either side and a whole crowd of crazies between me and my man.

Mine.

Because, shit, he *is* mine now. I can't lose him. And beyond that, I just can't bear to see him suffer. His pain is more important to me than my own, and I'll do anything to prevent it. I've already tried bargaining, offering my own services up for a death match to get Phoenix out of this. No such luck.

My eyes flick to the different exits in the room, wondering if there's some way I could cause a commotion or a stampede, *something* to distract these idiots long enough for me and Phoenix to run. That's all I'm asking. I'm not trying to be brave her or save the world. I know it's selfish, but there's only one man in this room that I care about saving.

*Codrick, give me strength,* I pray as I debate the chances of getting shot by either of these men. The crowd is thick and a bullet could really go anywhere in here. I imagine that they probably *wouldn't* shoot me. I mean, where do I have to go? No matter what I do, I'm not getting out of here without going through one of them. But what if I'm not trying to get out? What if I'm just trying to get … over there.

Around the corner from where I'm standing, there's a glass door that leads to an office. And just inside that … a red metal square with a handle. A fire alarm. There's a fucking fire alarm.

When I turn my attention back to Phoenix, he's taking a punch on the side of the face that makes my teeth hurt *for* him. He follows it up immediately with a blow that makes the other man stumble against the outer edge of the cage. He doesn't even get a chance to stand up before Phoenix is there, kicking him as hard as he can in the belly, making my own tummy hurt in sympathy. He doesn't want to be doing this, but he doesn't think he has a choice.

I'm going to give him one.

Phoenix pummels the other man with a wild fierceness, using every ounce of that protective nature of his to fight *for me*. He's fighting for me in there, not himself. And it's heartbreaking. He's strong and fierce, but he's a gentle fucking giant and I know this is killing him. Besides, even if he does win, what'll happen then? We'll be locked together in a room until his next fight, and his next, and his next? Until he dies or Roch gets tired of having to watch him. And then I'll be ... raped or sold or killed, too.

Nothing good is going to come out of this.

Closing my eyes against the sight of the carnage in that ring, I take several long, deep breaths and imagine that Codrick is right there beside me.

*"You can do this, Baby Girl,"* he tells me, smiling in that soft, easy way of his. *"I'm right here with you, okay? I'm right here."*

My lids open and I relax my hands from the tight fists they've been clenched into for hours. With the armed guards and the heaving crowd, with Phoenix trapped in the ring, I don't think Roch even considered tying me up. He doesn't think he needs to.

*Idiot.*

Before I think long enough to let the thought show on my face ... I just start running. I sprint toward that office as fast as I can, my whole focus on the fire alarm inside that door. I don't know if it'll be unlocked, if I'll be able to break the glass, but it's worth it a shot because it's the only one I've got.

A shot rings out from behind me, grazing my arm and making me hiss in pain as the bullet burns across my skin. I stumble, but I don't fall, picking myself up and throwing my entire body into the run. *They shot at me! They actually took a goddamn shot!* A second shot rings out and then a third, both missing me by a *hair* and slamming into the hard packed dirt beneath my feet.

One of the guards catches me, grabbing onto my arm and throwing me hard against the corrugate metal wall before he puts a hand to my throat.

"You stupid cunt," he growls out, but as he pins me there, I hear commotion and screaming, a stampede of footsteps punctuated with shouted curses and cries for help. Behind the guard's massive bulky form, I see people pushing and shoving, running for the exits as a man bleeds out on the ground, clutching at his chest, red blood bubbling from his lips.

I didn't make the fire alarm, but the shots have startled the crowd, set that mob mentality that Roch and his rich friends coaxed so well and turned it into a frenzy.

271

Somewhere in the distance, I hear Phoenix roaring my name, but my hands are clawing at the guards eyes, nails scraping along his face as my vision flickers and blurs. I slam a fist down on his elbow and for just a second, his grip lessens. It's enough for me to suck in a single gasping breath before Phoenix tackles him, knocking the asshole off me completely and onto the ground in front of me.

With wheezing breaths, I slide to the ground and try to focus, to bring myself back to the present. The crowd might be stampeding and Phoenix might be here fighting for me, but it won't last. Someone else with a gun will come; they'll get the crowd under control; I'll be in an even worse position than I started in.

Phoenix is wrestling with the man for control of gun, muscles bunching, blood dripping down the side of his face as he narrows those gray eyes on his new opponent, holding the guard's gun hand in a tight fist and using the other to punch him in the face not once, not twice, but three, four, five fucking times.

Pushing myself to my feet, I turn just in time to see another armed asshole with a gun moving toward us. I'm still wheezing and choking, so maybe he doesn't see me as a threat, but I tackle him before he can get to close to Phoenix, just as fierce and wild and protective of him as he is of me. The force and surprise of my small, mus-

cular body knocks the guard onto his ass. His gun flies out of his hand and across the floor, but as I go to grab it, *he* surprises me with this time by snatching my right ankle and yanking so hard that I fall.

In a second he's on top of me, hitting me in the face as hard as he can, giving me stars behind my flickering eyelids. He raises his fist to hit me again when Phoenix wraps an inked, muscular arm around his throat and squeezes hard, knocking the man out and tossing him to the side like garbage.

"C'mere, Baby Girl," he chokes out, bleeding and shaking and sweating. He yanks me to my feet and we start running for the exit, blending into the crowd. I don't have to worry about being run over because Phoenix is so goddamn big and imposing.

Without waiting to see what's going to happen with the panicking crowd, we head right for the edge of the swamp, the dark waters beckoning like an old friend. I'm not nearly as scared of the bayou as I am of what's happening behind us.

But we don't make it to the water because Roch is suddenly there with *four* huge fucking men.

"Alright," he says, pulling the hammer back on his gun and using two steady hands to lift it to Phoenix's face. "I'm done with this shit; you're a fucking liability." Slowly, carefully, he turns the weapon from Phoenix … to me.

In a movement so fast I barely register it, Phoenix shoves me out of the way and just *barely* manages to avoid getting shot.

"Oh, for fuck's sake, this is pathetic." Roch turns to the two of us lying on the ground, Phoenix's massive body on top of and in front of mine, and he reaches for the trigger.

"I love you so much, Baby Girl. So much. So goddamn much," Phoenix says, and I feel his muscles tensing for one last fight.

"I love you, too," I choke out, knowing that in seconds, we'll both be shot. We'll be dead. And it'll all be over.

*"At least we'll get to see other again,"* I tell Codrick's ghost, but he's already shaking his head.

*"Not yet,"* he whispers, and then there are blue and red lights, black vans, men with guns.

Phoenix stiffens up and puts his arm out to keep me down as Roch turns, weapon in hand, to the horde of police or federal agents or SWAT or whatever the fuck they are.

And as we sit there in complete and total shock, a gun goes off and Roch's head explodes in red.

■ ■ ■ ■ ■ ■ ■ ■ ■ ■ ■ ■

"Holy shit!" Priya is saying, panting as we're escorted to the edge of the dirt parking lot where she's standing. I'm surprised to see her there, but Phoenix doesn't seem to be.

"How you get all these uniforms out here so quick?" he asks as I cock a brow and he smiles softly. "I dialed her before they took my phone," he adds and my mouth parts in surprise. Damn. Good thinking.

"More than that," she says, giving Phoenix a hug and then, without hesitation, she gives me one, too. "When I was at that stoplight, I got your call and glanced in the rearview. I saw that asshole in the white truck get out with a gun." She levels a look on Phoenix as an officer watches over us and others scurry around gathering up what's left of the crowd.

I doubt all of the ones that splashed into the swamp to escape arrest are going to get as lucky as me and Phoenix. If you don't know your way around out there, you're screwed. *Fuck 'em.* I hope they get eaten by gators.

"You know my dad's head of state police, right?" Priya asks, putting a hand on her hip. "I have favors to call in when I need them."

"This is more than just a favor," I say, looking around at the ambulances, the cop cars, the unmarked vans. A shiver trails down my spine. Fuck, this is a lot bigger than I first thought, but as I step close to Phoenix and curl my fingers with his ... I'm not sure that I care. The only thing that matters to me is right here. Turning, I press my forehead against his arm and lean in close.

"Maybe," Priya admits, her voice softening as she watches us together. I can feel Phoenix's big hand on my head, ruffling up my hair. He saved my life tonight. And I saved his, too, maybe? I think we might be even. "There's more to this than I'm privy to, unfortunately." She lifts her head up and smiles at someone behind us. "But I will talk to my dad and see if I can't give you a ride. I know where you live after all." She wiggles her eyebrows as moves away.

"You okay down dere?" Phoenix asks, turning to face me and pulling me into his arms for one of those perfect fucking hugs of his.

"I'm just fine," I tell him, leaning back and looking up into those beautiful gray eyes. Pretty sure I'm still numb with shock, but ... that little figment of imagination I was talking to as Codrick ... he was right.

One day we'll see him again.

One day, just not today.

"As long as I'm with you," I add, pressing my cheek to Phoenix's chest and closing my eyes as I listen to the beautiful, rhythmic sound of his heartbeat.

He's alive … and so am I. And as long as I have those two things, everything else is a problem that can be fixed.

# EMBRY

## EPILOGUE

Phoenix and I sit on a blanket with a picnic basket next to us, camped out in the grassy area in front of Codrick's final resting place. Might seem like a weird place to have a picnic, but that's the thing with grief and loss. Everybody processes it differently. There are no right answers and what seems weird or whiny or fucked-up or morbid to some ... is really just a part of the healing process for everyone else.

"You don't mine me sleepin' wit' your girl, right?" Phoenix asks, lifting up a glass of champagne in salute toward Codrick's tomb, the Landry name carved into the stone with big block letters. The white surface of the crypt shimmers in the sunshine, a sparkle, almost like laughter in response to Phoenix's stupid joke.

I elbow him in the side, but his muscles are like rocks and it doesn't seem to faze him much.

"I can't believe I moved back here to be with you," I mumble under my breath, casting a narrow-eyed glare in his direction. That's a lie, of course. I decided to move back here for a whole number of reasons. The first of which ... was for me. I wasn't happy in New York. It was the place I ran to when I couldn't take the pain and the memories. It was an escape that was never meant to be permanent.

Living with Phoenix Benoit in the swamp is a little ... weird. Weird, but fucking awesome. Because, you know, sex. My stuff should be arriving soon, and as soon as the new semester rolls around, I'm starting at a new school. The only thing left I had to do to finish up my classes in NYU ... was send that grief paper.

Now that that's over and done with ... I can do things like this, hang out with Phoenix and Codrick the way I've always done.

"If he were here right now, he'd pinch your nipple," I grumble, taking a drink of my own champagne and wondering what the occasion is. Beyond, the obvious I mean, of coming here and placing a few small trinkets at the foot of Codrick's grave. I'm taking them all back home with me when we're done, but I thought he might want to see his favorite hoodie, the key to his house he gave me sophomore year of high school, and some weird gris-gris charm that Phoenix made for him.

"Nah, he'd be *much* more interested in pinching your nipple," Phoenix growls, his gray eyes meeting mine and sending a sharp thrill through me.

"Wouldn't work," I whisper, downing the last of my drink and holding my glass out for another refill. My head feels light and bubbly, and I'm glad we only have to walk back to Wings of Fire and Ash after this. No fucking way would I let either of us drive. Sorry, but I'm a hard-ass. One drop of alcohol and it's a no. Codrick wasn't intoxicated when he crashed—we might never know *why* he crashed—but I don't care. Anything to make driving safer, that's what we're going to do. "I'd just moan instead."

Phoenix gives me a wolfish grin, dressed in a red tank that used to be Codrick's draped in ink that's fully and completely his. Turning my left wrist over, I take a look at my first tattoo, the one I got just yesterday that still stings like a bitch. It's a bit funky because it's still fresh, but I don't care. The words *RIP CODRICK* have never brought me such comfort before. Because I know if he's watching me now, he can finally take a deep breath and rest, relax, move on if he has to … Phoenix and I, we're going to be okay.

"You would, wouldn't you?" Phoenix growls, leaning forward to give me a kiss. The ring of my finger clinks against the glass in my hand, and I know that someday soon, we'll discuss it more. But for right now, this is okay, this is perfect, and it's exactly where we need to be. "Disturb all dem ghosts wit' your moaning."

I smile against his mouth, pressing close and breathing in that musky, spicy, minty scent of him. There's nothing like it in the world, and it's wholly and completely mine. I rest a hand on Phoenix's bicep and look into his eyes as he pulls away, studying me with his stormy gaze.

"I love you," I whisper before the moment gets too intense and I find those words even more embarrassing to say. But I've seen how life can throw curveballs you don't expect, and I refuse to ever regret *not* saying them. The last words Codrick ever sent me were …

Phoenix fills in the thought for me, kissing me hard and fierce on the mouth, tasting of passion and perseverance and second chances.

"I love you, Baby Girl," he whispers as the wind blows gently, tousling my hair and teasing my cheek, Codrick's ghostly fingers saying goodbye … and good luck.

# Tasting Never

AMAZON BESTSELLING AUTHOR
C.M. STUNICH

The Tasting Never Series, Book 1

"Never Ross wants to be loved. It's that simple, but it's not that easy."

# 1

Rick is a perfectly nice guy.

But not for me.

Rick is the kind of guy you can take home to your family, show off, and know that at the end of the day, he'll be there for you. I'm not into guys like Rick. I should be, but I'm not. I think there's something wrong with me. I need a guy like Rick to put me on the straight and narrow, to help me stop doing the things I shouldn't be doing and start doing the things I should.

Right now, my back is to a wall and I'm kissing the neck of a guy I don't know. My therapist says it's because I have 'daddy' issues. Like that's supposed to mean something to me. How can I have daddy issues when I barely knew the prick? He didn't walk out on me and mom like my therapist thinks. She thinks that because I've never told her the truth. My dad died right in front of my eyes, called out my name seconds before the light went out of his face and left him cold. That's all I remember about him. Other than that, my mind is a blank, a series of shadowy pictures without words. They don't make any fucking sense.

The guy I'm kissing unbuttons his pants. I think about telling him to use a condom, but I just don't feel like it. I'm on the pill anyway. He thrusts into me while I'm watching Rick through a crack in the door. He's drinking punch, not alcohol, and smiling with big, wide teeth in a face that's handsome, but not too handsome. Rick's the kind of guy that your friends compliment you on, tell you he's gorgeous, but they never try to sleep with him. The ones they really want, the dangerous ones, the ones with pasts that burn like fire and melt everything around them … Those are the guys that I always seem to fall for. The one I'm having sex with right now is one of those. I don't even know his name.

"I love you," the guy says over and over, and I roll my eyes. I've heard it before, a hundred times, and I just don't want to hear it anymore. I pretend to have an orgasm, moaning and groaning and scratching his back, and all the while, I'm watching Rick. We have a date

tomorrow night that I think I'm going to cancel. I thought maybe I'd take Rick out, see how chivalrous he really was, but tonight, he's wearing khaki pants and a red sweater. I don't date guys like Rick.

The guy I'm fucking finishes and tells me how great I am. Then he disappears and I don't see him again, not that night or any other. I light a cigarette and leave the room before any of the drunken idiots at the party stumble in and find me there with my panties around my ankles. I step out of them and stuff them in my pocket, aware that my skirt is too short and that my ass is hanging out. I just can't seem to find it in myself to care.

"Hey," Rick says, intercepting me before I can reach the front door. "We still on for tomorrow night?" He looks me up and down, and I can see that he's curious about my disheveled appearance, my mussy hair and my swollen lips, but he doesn't ask about it. I don't think he even gives it a second thought. Rick doesn't know that girls like me exist. He's heard about them on TV, maybe even masturbates to them, but he doesn't really believe that they exist in this world or any other. I really should keep my date with Rick, go out with him, and grow up.

"I can't," I say, biting my lip seductively and touching his cashmere sweater with a shaking hand. I don't know why it's shaking, but I don't like it, so I pull it back and let it fall to my side. I blow cigarette smoke in Rick's face which is rude, but that I do anyway. There's a monster inside of me, eating little bits of me everyday, and I can't seem to stop it. It makes me do things I don't want to do, say things I don't want to say. It makes me tell Rick that I've got to study for a test that he really believes I have.

I kiss him on the lips and leave an orange-red stain before I walk out the door and down the front steps. People wave at me as I go by and say they'll see me around, but I don't really know who any of them are, so I avoid their stares and their friendly smiles. It's all fake, just a big load of shit that I can't buy into or I'll die. If I ever believe in something again, and it turns out to be false, then not only will my body crumble beneath me, but so will my soul. I'll disintegrate, disappear into the wind and blow away. I'll be nothing. I'll blank out and the energy of who I was will just go away, melt into the ground and come back as something unimportant, like a dandelion or a caterpillar. I can't find it in my heart to care.

I walk back to the dorms because I don't have a car. My roommate isn't home which doesn't surprise me. She's in love with another girl, one that's straight as an arrow. They have sleepovers in her dorm room and 'practice' kissing one another like they're in high school or something. That's fine with me because it means I

have the room all to myself, gives me a chance to be alone. I feel most comfortable that way. When you're alone, there's nobody there to hurt you or let you down. It feels too good to have that guarantee of solitude.

I fall on my back on the bed and try to breathe through the tears that come to me unbidden. I don't want them, never asked for them. I couldn't even tell you what I was crying over or why. I just do. Every night, I lay here and I try to find something in myself to live for. Every night, I fail and wonder if I need a guy like Rick to show me the way. But then, I'm a big girl, and a feminist, too, so why do I think a guy could save my soul?

I never thought to wonder if I was looking at it the wrong way, if maybe it wasn't a guy that I was looking for, just a person. And maybe I didn't need them to save my soul, just to give me the other half of it. Maybe that was it?

## KEEP UP WITH ALL THE FUN ... AND EARN SOME FREE BOOKS!

JOIN THE C.M. STUNICH NEWSLETTER – Get three free books just for signing up http://eepurl.com/DEsEf

TWEET ME ON TWITTER, BABE – Come sing the social media song with me https://twitter.com/CMStunich

SNAPCHAT WITH ME – Get exclusive behind the scenes looks at covers, blurbs, book signings and more http://www.snapchat.com/add/cmstunich

LISTEN TO MY BOOK PLAYLISTS – Share your fave music with me and I'll give you my playlists (I'm super active on here!) https://open.spotify.com/user/CMStunich

FRIEND ME ON FACEBOOK – Okay, I'm actually at the 5,000 friend limit, but if you click the "follow" button on my profile page, you'll see way more of my killer posts https://facebook.com/cmstunich

CHECK OUT THE NEW SITE – (under construction) but it looks kick-a$$ so far, right? You can order signed books here! http://www.cmstunich.com

READ VIOLET BLAZE – Read the books from my hot as hellfire pen name, Violet Blaze http://www.violetblazebooks.com

SUBSCRIBE TO MY RSS FEED – Press that little orange button in the corner and copy that RSS feed so you can get all the latest updates http://www.cmstunich.com/blog

AMAZON, BABY – If you click the follow button here, you'll get an email each time I put out a new book. Pretty sweet, huh? http://amazon.com/author/cmstunich
http://amazon.com/author/violetblaze

PINTEREST – Lots of hot half-naked men. Oh, and half-naked men. Plus, tattooed guys holding babies (who are half-naked) http://pinterest.com/cmstunich

INSTAGRAM – Cute cat pictures. And half-naked guys. Yep, that again. http://instagram.com/cmstunich

GRAB A SMOKIN' HOT READ – Check out my books, grab one or two or five. Fall in love over and over again. Satisfaction guaranteed, baby. ;)

AMAZONhttp://amazon.com/author/cmstunich
B&Nhttp://tinyurl.com/cmbarnes
iTUNEShttp://tinyurl.com/cmitunesbooks
GOOGLE PLAYhttp://tinyurl.com/cmgoogle
KOBOhttp://tinyurl.com/cmkobobooks
VIOLET BLAZEhttp://amazon.com/author/violetblaze

P.S. I heart the f*ck out of you! Thanks for reading! I love your faces.
<3 C.M. Stunich aka Violet Blaze

## ABOUT THE AUTHOR

C.M. Stunich is a self-admitted bibliophile with a love for exotic teas and a whole host of characters who live full time inside the strange, swirling vortex of her thoughts. Some folks might call this crazy, but Caitlin Morgan doesn't mind – especially considering she has to write biographies in the third person. Oh, and half the host of characters in her head are searing hot bad boys with dirty mouths and skillful hands (among other things). If being crazy means hanging out with them everyday, C.M. has decided to have herself committed.

She hates tapioca pudding, loves to binge on cheesy horror movies, and is a slave to many cats. When she's not vacuuming fur off of her couch, C.M. can be found with her nose buried in a book or her eyes glued to a computer screen. She's the author of over thirty novels – romance, new adult, fantasy, and young adult included. Please, come and join her inside her crazy. There's a heck of a lot to do there.

Oh, and Caitlin loves to chat (incessantly), so feel free to e-mail her, send her a Facebook message, or put up smoke signals. She's already looking forward to it.